THE UNDER GROOVE

THE UNDER GROOVE

ARTHUR STRINGER

Originally published in 1912.
Published by Wildside Press LLC.
Visit us online at wildsidepress.com

CHAPTER ONE
THE ADVENTURE OF THE THIRD ARM

I

It wasn't until Dinney and I had divvied our swag that I wanted to travel eastward. But I always weaken on the West that way, especially when I've got money.

I never could say just how or why it was. Besides, there were too many things, in this erratic life of mine, that were over-hard to explain away. It seemed to have no beginning and no end. It led nowhere. Time and time again I seemed to have dug down to the bed-rock where the "fault" lay, but each time, as I tunnelled and sifted deeper and deeper into Consciousness, some sudden mountain freshet of Memory swept everything from me. So I accepted life as the heap of tailings it was, as the rubble it had proved.

Yet across the fog of uncertainty through which I moved could always be made out a city between two rivers, a hurrying and huddled and harlequin-hearted city, which, while it sucked you into its vortex, at least tossed and tumbled you out of your own moodiness.

I wanted to go East. Most dogs, I suppose, go home to bury their bone. And I always turned sour when I wasn't on the move. So I began to get homesick and peevish for New York. I wanted to sniff the familiar old ferry smell, to hear the rush and gutter of water in the narrowing slips where the piling yields and shudders against the bumping paddle-boxes, to catch the metallic and familiar *tink-a-link* of pawl-and-ratchets as the landing-floats lower to crowded deck-lips. I ached for a sight of that old crust-thrower of a town, where its sky-scraper teeth bit up into the morning smoke, and it seemed to whisper, with one eye winked: "Feed me, or I'll feed on you!" I wanted to see it laugh and shake behind its sly old rags. I wanted to hear its eternal whine for more gold, its growls and oaths against the arm of the law. I wanted to get a sniff of the Rialto dust again, of the crowds by day and the lamps by night, of the bustle and stir of Broadway, with its crazy and solemn and tangled and happy-go-lucky bubbling of life. My ears seemed to ache for its street-sounds,

1

its roar of wheels, its clatter of hoofs, its clangour and pulse of bells, its whine of engines, its drone of power, its show of wealth, its rumble and roar of Hunger.

"I want it all, Dinney!" I said to that puzzled son of the Sucker State, who knew nothing of life or living beyond the range of the Hoosiers. "I want it all, from the Greek peanut-man with his barrel-oven and his little steam-whistle to the flash of the afternoon sun on some wine-coloured tonneau as it dips and melts away up the Avenue! I want it all, from the old Irish newswomen and the passing street-faces, and the nighthawks of the Tenderloin to the groups of well-built and bright-eyed girls in velvet and feathers and furs, with muffs as big as cash-boxes, Dinney, and bunches of violets the size of a cabbage—the girls who come laughing and talking down Fifth Avenue every afternoon and make me wish I'd kept out of the Under Groove and stuck to honest ways!"

"Aw, cut it out!" growled Dinney.

"Yes, I want it all," I mused, looking down on Dinney, the illiterate, from the throne of my rhapsody, "from the signs of the Bowery to those big hotel-names that are stippled in electrics, and the theatres that are spangled with circles and fountains of light, and the glow of rose and gold that hangs over that river-bed of unrest which is forever known to us as Broadway!"

"Aw, slush!" said Dinney, in disgust.

Yet Dinney had his good points. Among others, he was not over-inquisitive. He never nagged after my record. He never alluded to me as a Man of Mystery. Once and once only had he mildly inquired just how I had happened to drop down into the ways of the Under Groove: that was the day, in Chicago, when we had watched a patrolman club a mulatto stuss-worker on the head. The first sickening blow of that nightstick had turned my very soul over in its cage; and Dinney had the unique and altogether unexpected experience of beholding me go flat down on the sidewalk, in a dead faint. And it must have puzzled him a bit, for he knew I was not a coward. Yet he called the incident closed, when he saw how I felt, without harassing me with any third-degree hold-ups. He was willing to let by-gones be by-gones. He sometimes felt the difference in our worldly standing, I think, but it never affected his faithfulness, for Dinney was never a welcher. Nor had he ever stood afraid of anything this side of the Eternal. But Dinney had started wrong. He'd begun his career under William Rudolph, alias "The Missouri Kid," had dawdled along as a hobo stick-up, and had finally climbed up to the Yegg class under the guidance and inspiration of Buck Ballard, of the Goat Hinch Band.

So Dinney, naturally, was uncouth of speech and crude of feeling. When he snuffed a drum, it was for the money in it, and nothing more. He never saw any fun in the game for the game's sake. He never even had the heart to go it alone. He was menial; he always had to work under somebody, had Dinney. He was not a coward in body, for he would have waded and slashed his way out ear-deep in blood if he'd ever been cornered. But he was a coward in mind, in spirit; he had even shivered and turned sick when I made him walk into a Decatur bank and pass through a ridiculous little raised check. He had fallen into a rut, and he had to stick to that rut, or he wasn't happy.

And that's where we differed! And that's why he kept to his Middle West and drifted down St. Louis and Memphis way, until he could get into touch with Janesville Tommy or come under the wing of Big Jim Stratton. For three weeks I tried to do my best with Dinney, for I liked him. But I'd nothing to work on. A man who hasn't a soul above moll-buzzing is hopeless. So Dinney and I divvied on the Pontiac *coup*, and parted.

It had been a neat little piece of business, that Pontiac *coup*. Dinney and a broken-down pick-up named Sherwood, who'd pounded the brass on one of the Chicago pool-room barges, trailed out along the Chicago and Alton until they were twelve miles north of the town. I'd shown Sherwood how to cut in on one of the Pontiac wires, with our relays and batteries stowed away behind a pile of ties. Once we'd dug out and connected with the right wires we controlled every message that passed between the Windy City and Livingston County. I carried through the inside work myself, working the town as a hog-buyer from Milwaukee and "spreading" at the best hotel. Then I floated into one of the town banks—it was the Livingston and Illinois Investor's—flagging a Chicago draft for six thousand four hundred dollars. I gave them the Chicago bank for reference, and when they still held back, I told them to wire at my expense. And wire they did.

They wired into Sherwood's relay, behind a pile of ties, twelve miles out on the Chicago and Alton. And while that half-fed old pool-room tout was sending back his message, to the effect that I was all right and as good as gold, I sat in the lobby of my hotel, reading a chapter or two of Balzac. I sauntered over to the bank again when they 'phoned for me. I knew, as I faced that cashier, that one of two things was there within three feet of me, waiting for me—either a pile of bills, or a pair of handcuffs. Dinney, I suppose, would have shown just how he felt. I rather think I showed nothing but annoyance, and when that cashier flung the six thousand four hundred out through the little wicket at me, I pushed half of the pile back and asked for smaller denominations. Then I recounted my roll, thanked him, and sauntered back to the hotel. But once I'd rounded the corner of that hotel, I could have shown a clean pair of heels to a lightning-change artist between acts.

II

I felt that it was good to be back in New York. My heart went out to it, like a hobo's hand to a schooner-shank. I drowsed and revelled in it all, even as I felt it harry and hammer and batter me into a sort of partial anæsthesia of indifferency. But most of all I loved that dark and attenuated cavern of Speed, that slender tunnel of pulsing twilight, the Subway, where Unrest meteored past its tiers of wire-strung lights and the air hung alive and tremulous with its passion of hurry.

So I stood there contentedly, swaying from a car-strap, satisfied with the drone of the train, catching fleeting glimpses of the polished track-rails as they flashed back silver-white above the head-light glimmer. I forgot the fetid smell of car-oil and thrice-breathed air, touched into vague wonder as I was at the thought of thus cannonading about under the very floor of the great teeming City, a little tickled, too, at the consciousness that even subterranean movement could be made majestic.

With one hand, as I have said, I clung to the car-strap. With the other I held my evening paper. I let my eye run indolently down its column of racing-returns. I had just made note, in the Benning's track news, that Rippling Water had finished first in the fifth event for three-year-olds, and had built up an equally lazy picture, in my mind's eye, of the big mare romping down the home-stretch, when

4

an almost nameless something sent a shock, as distinct as the tingle of an electric current, through my body.

I did not betray this shock by any outward sign. But as the crowded Subway express rocked and swayed along its rails I let my half-closed eyes coast first to the right and then to the left. This I did without a movement of the head or a lowering of the paper before my face.

On one side of me was an obese and bearded German, deep in the day's market reports. On the other was a young woman of twenty-one or two. Her left hand, gloved in black, clung to a strap. Her right hand hung at her side, lost in a huge black lynx muff. Packed in about us were scores of strap-hangers like myself, lulled into child-like quiescence by their cradling and appeasing nurse of speed. But with the exception of this man and woman no one in the car stood within actual reaching distance of me.

I let my well-guarded glance shift back to the young woman's face, without so much as moving my head. It seemed an impassive and preoccupied face, and its pallor was the most striking thing about it. Yet it was a soft and ivory sort of pallor, too white to be called olive. It was made more remarkable by the shadows under the moody and impersonal eyes, and by the deep red of the lips, which drooped a little at the corners, petulantly, like those of a woman who had known too much of sickness, or had rebelled too fiercely against it. Beyond this she seemed a well-poised and well-groomed American girl, with that air of mild and fragile beauty which may come, I know, sometimes from too much tea, and sometimes from too much Huyler's. Her hat was a wide Gainsborough, with heavy plumes. The lynx boa, that hung over her smart-looking shoulder-cape of black broadcloth, was heavy and costly. But what interested me most, even at that moment, was the little Lalique pendant of pigeon-blood rubies she wore at her throat. There were twelve of them, surrounding a *pendeloque* of startling size and clarity. The rubies themselves, which were even more beautiful stones, were held together by the slenderest woven chain of Roman gold. And I could not help speculating how one quick little movement of the fingers, in a crowded car like that, might make away with thirteen stones that would bring a thousand, perhaps two thousand, dollars from any dealer in New York.

Then suddenly up and down the middle of my back I once more felt that minute tingling sensation which arises only at the acutest nervous shock. It was a mental start, like the reactional movement of a hand on which a spark of fire had fallen. I felt, for a moment, as though a thousand little icicles had danced along my spinal column.

For the girl who was standing so quietly and impassively beside me was deliberately, guardedly, but unmistakably, feeling my pocket.

III

My first feeling, when the wonder of the thing had passed, was an incongruous and unholy joy in the irony of the situation. Here was an old and experienced dip and box man, an airy-handed *chevalier d'industrie*, an ex-yegg, being quietly held up by a sugar-and-milk slip of a girl! Here was a pink-and-white china doll giving the dare to an Under Groove adventurer who had once faced Doogan and all his forces! It was worth losing an eight-dollar watch, just for a chance to see the game.

Have you ever watched a bottle of *Spumante* with the cork drawn? Or a half-emptied seltzer-siphon when the pressure is first removed? Well, that's what I was like at this sudden discovery. The repression of weeks, the burden of being quiescent and slothfully decent, was a thing of the past. The pressure of a too-confining moral atmosphere was lifted. I seemed to bubble and effervesce with a rioting return of spirits. I found myself suddenly exhilarated and challenged by the old and inalienable quest of adventure. It even left me indifferent to the bad air and steel-dust of the Subway. It left me face to face with the old predatory life again. And I stood there almost revelling in it all, inwardly cautioning myself to go slow and be watchful.

I first let my absent and innocent gaze go up to the row of advertising cards above the car windows, where hair-fluids and face-balms and nerve-pills and parasitic knick-knacks and nostrums shouted down their insistence on being acknowledged as essentials of life. Then I glanced, half-diffidently, at the girl herself. She seemed so self-immured, so unconscious of her surroundings, so pensive and timid-looking about the shadowy eyes, that a moment of uncertainty came back to me. Yet even as I doubted I could feel that cautiously exploring hand push deeper in under my coat, as softly as a snake's head under a leaf.

I buried my face behind my paper and peered to the right. The obese German, still wrapped in his market reports, was beyond question. The woman, and the woman alone, stood within reaching distance of me. I looked back at her, guardedly, over the top of my paper. Her left hand, in its long, black, kid glove, was lifted high above her head, clinging to the car-strap. I moved my paper inch by inch with the jolting of the car, until I commanded a view of her right arm. I could see it hanging inert and motionless at her side, the full sweep of it, right down to where the gloved fingers were lost in the depth of the huge fur muff it carried.

Then still again that feeling of a thousand dancing icicles crept up and down my backbone. For even while I saw her two hands, the one above clinging to the strap, the other hanging at her side, holding the muff, I felt the cautious movements of the exploring fingers under my coat. Yet those fingers could belong to no one but the woman beside me.

But there, before me, as clear as light, I could see both her own hands. I could also see the cloth of my coat rise and fall with the little movements of some slender and agile wrist. I could feel the padding fingers still delicately groping, advancing, searching. And the truth flashed on me, with a shock that was almost sickening. It was neither illusion nor mistake. But it was an arm, with five flexible and living fingers at its end. Through some monstrous affliction or accident *the woman standing at my side was the possessor of a third hand*!

IV

It was no easy thing for me to control myself. But I made it a point to see that not a sign, not a tremor, escaped me, as I felt those uncanny and restless fingers loosen my chain and slowly lift the watch from where it nestled in my left-hand waistcoat pocket. It was done with the unerring precision of an expert.

I felt, as I stood there beside that motionless and tranquil body in black broadcloth, that the tentacle of an octopus had darted out and was threatening me. There seemed something unhuman, revolting, sickening, in the thought of this third mysterious member, so endowed with malignant and predaceous life, padding and exploring about my body. It was like calmly enduring the crawling of a serpent. I felt as though the woman beside me was something reptilious and pre-Adamitic, some secretive-minded, many-membered monstrosity of paleolithic times. It took a struggle to keep from crowding and tearing away from her touch.

I saw the fingered tentacle slowly recede, inch by inch. It seemed to draw back into nothingness behind the black lynx boa. But with it, of course, it carried my watch and chain. No other portion of the woman's body moved. She hung there immobile, amid the universal swaying of the car. She might have been carved in marble, she stood so calm and meditative, with the empty, unseeing eyes of a statue. Then I noticed that the tentacle was once more creeping and stealing out in my direction. I half-lowered my paper, with a little unconcerned yawn of weariness. As I did so the extended tentacle flashed back into its muffling gloom. It seemed to me terribly like the movement of some frightened devilfish, drawing an arm back into its sheltering cave.

When the crowd ebbed from the car at the Grand Central Station I was glad enough for a momentary escape into one of the empty cross-seats. The woman remained where she was, merely sinking into a seat near the door. I was possessed by a ridiculous and irrational fear of her. I wanted to think things over at my leisure, to digest my discovery, as soldiers, it is said, must digest victory.

But first, to make sure my watch was indeed gone, I surreptitiously felt in the pocket of my waistcoat.

No watch was there. Nor was there one jot of silver left in my change pocket. But what almost brought me to my feet, with a gasp of incredulous astonishment, was the amazing discovery that my pigskin wallet, holding in all some six hundred dollars in bills, had been taken, under my very eyes, from the breast-pocket of my coat.

This discovery showed me that I had something more than thinking to do. It was necessity now, and no longer caprice, that governed my return to the feral state. It was for something more than the game for the game's sake that this mystery would have to be sought out to its bitterest end. Whatever its meaning, I felt, as I studied the calm and unbetraying woman with the black muff, I was at least facing an adventurer quite as artful and audacious as myself.

V

When the train stopped at Seventy-second Street the woman hurriedly left the car and mounted to the street. I watched her, circumspectly, from the back platform. Then I followed her at what I thought a safe distance.

Night had already fallen when I emerged from the Subway, and it was by the electric lamps of upper Broadway that I made out the already familiar figure hurrying westward toward the river. At West End Avenue she turned sharply north, on the west side. By the time I had rounded the corner she was well up this avenue, but still plainly in sight. So I kept shadowing her, block by block, as she hurried along that quiet and undulating street of placid-fronted homes. She looked back once, and only once; as she did so I made it a point to be stooping over a street-corner letter-box. Then I saw her run up a short flight of house-steps and a moment later disappear through a door.

I walked on, past the house, for a moment's reconnaissance. Then, I guardedly studied the place with its little plot of grass, its three sickly maples, its darkened windows, its tangle of wistaria vines that crept to the very roof-cornice—studied it very much as you would study a pile of stones under which a cobra had slipped. It flashed through my mind, inappositely, as I peered up and down the quiet street, at those unbetraying stone faces before so many hidden homes, how well masked behind brick and stone and mortar the sorrows and mysteries and romances of any great city must always remain. Then I realized that I was losing time, and that my only line of advance could be by direct assault. So I swung about and ran up the steps without further delay.

No answer came to my impatient ring. I pushed the electric button a second time, more angrily, pondering how I should explain myself, speculating what my procedures should be if I were indeed denied admittance, comprehending for the first time the predicament into which I had so unwittingly drifted.

As I did so the door slowly opened and an old butler, in claret-coloured livery, stood before me. He stood peering out at me, with bent shoulders and snow-white hair, one hand behind his ear, as a sign, I took it, that he was hard of hearing. His eyes, I noticed, were dim and haggard, like a mastiff's. His fine old face, however, was

9

far from being either canine or servile in its quiet dignity. Indeed, he was on the point of shutting the door in my face when I stepped quickly forward.

This left my body between the jamb and the door-edge. The outcome might have been disagreeable, to say the least, had not a second figure suddenly appeared behind him.

It was that of a woman of thirty, in the striped blue and white uniform of a trained nurse. Out of a face that was too keenly intelligent to be imperious, and so strongly lined, as to be almost manlike, looked a pair of alert and tragic and yet unhardened eyes. In fact, this troubled look of tragedy impressed me still further as she waved the bent old butler to one side, and, a little curtly, a little apprehensively, asked me my business.

The old butler disappeared like a shadow beyond the gloom of the unlighted lower hall. But as he did so, high beyond the head of the waiting nurse, I caught one fleeting glimpse of a girlish figure in a black lynx boa, crossing at the top of the stairway. The woman at the door studied my face with a sudden look of open suspicion.

"I should like to see you alone, at once," I said to her. She bowed her head gravely, with a motion for me to enter. I could see the vague look of fear, however, that had leaped into her face.

VI

She ushered me into a well-furnished library, unlighted except by the open wood fire. She turned back, I noticed, to close the door.

"Has anything happened?" she demanded. Our eyes met combatively.

"Yes," I answered. And still she waited. "Two minutes ago a young woman entered this house."

The nurse responded with her grave and non-committal bow of the head.

"I must see that young woman, at once."

"May I not speak for her?" asked the woman in the uniform. Still again our eyes met, and some guarded look of appeal made the question, through all its coldness of tone, almost a supplication. From somewhere above stairs, as we stood there confronting each other, burst forth the sound of singing, as light and untroubled as a bird's. It was the voice of a young woman, joyous, innocent, ingenuous.

There was not a word spoken as we listened. But as the watching nurse took in my start of surprise I again saw some shadow of fear and foreboding creep across her face.

"I must see this young woman alone!" I insisted. The trained nurse took a deep breath, as though steeling herself for some ordeal.

"Are you a detective?" she suddenly asked me.

I told her I was not.

"Are you a newspaper reporter?"

That, too, I could truthfully disclaim. But I insisted on my right to see her. The nurse was sorry, but it was impossible.

"I not only must see your mistress, but I must see her at once, this minute!" There was no use beating further about the bush.

"She is not my mistress," corrected the woman before me quietly.

"Then what is she?" I asked in wonder.

The answer came in a lower tone, that was not without pregnancy:

"She is my patient."

Again, from without, I heard the sound of singing. It came nearer and nearer, and was followed by the clicking of high little shoe-heels on a polished wooden floor.

The nurse, with a little gasp of despair, ran to the door and turned the key in the lock. She did not face me until the singing voice had passed to the rear of the house, returned, and again ascended the stairway to the quick click of hurrying shoe-heels.

"*Who is that woman?*" I suddenly cried out, exasperated. As I did so I strode angrily toward the door, determined to fling it open and have done with all this quibbling over uncertainties.

The nurse barred my way. I could see the sudden fierce spirit of guardianship that had taken possession of her. It suggested to me the desperate animal passion of the she-bear determined to protect her invaded lair.

"That woman is nothing to you," she said quietly, though her voice shook.

"But I intend to be something to *her*!" I flung out, reckless of consequences now, and tired of all this mysteriousness into which I had floundered.

"What do you mean by that?" cried the nurse.

"I mean that I have every reason to believe the woman who just went up that stairway is a thief!"

"How dare you say that!"

"And I mean that you are deliberately standing between her and me in what you know to be a crime!"

"Oh, how dare you!" panted the nurse. Her face, by this time, was as white as chalk. "How dare you say that!"

"I dare say it because not half an hour ago she robbed me—because I saw her do it with my own eyes—because I followed her to this house and saw her come in the door that I came in."

The light was dim, but I did not fail to notice the uniformed figure before me suddenly begin to breathe hard and quick.

"*The woman who went up those stairs, the woman you heard singing, is not the woman who robbed you!*" she cried.

"What do you mean by that?"

"I mean that the woman you followed into this house is no longer here," was the reply.

"I don't believe you!"

She peered about her desperately, like some cornered animal seeking a final path of escape.

"You *must* believe me!" she cried foolishly, weakly. Through the dim light I could see that a sudden gush of tears had come to her eyes.

"Do you suppose I'm here to quibble about what I'm going to believe or not?" I demanded, unmoved by her tears. "I say I saw that woman come into this house."

The nurse, who had been torturing her handkerchief between her nervous fingers, suddenly clenched her hands. Then she looked me straight in the face.

"*There were two women came into this house when she came in!*"

VII

I stared at her, amazed, momentarily stupefied. My first impression was that I had blundered into a madhouse, that all the sober and solemn world about me had become a world of

12

delirium. Yet she looked sane and intelligent enough as she stood there confronting me, with her interlocked fingers pressed tightly together. I made a step toward her, and she fell back a step.

"What are you talking about?" I cried out at her. "What the devil do you mean by juggling phrases under my nose when you know what I'm here for and *I* know what I'm going to get before I leave?"

"I'm juggling no phrases," she retorted. "All I know is that you forced your way into a respectable household, and that you are making charges against a young woman of spotless reputation, a girl of wealth and social standing who——"

"Who is not above picking a pocket in a crowded car!" I cut in on her.

"Oh!" she cried, in a tremulous little gasp, putting her hand up to her heart.

"Who calmly, deliberately, stole six hundred dollars from my coat-pocket!" I went on, letting loose my dammed-up torrent of rage. My eye had caught the glimmer of light on the nickel of a desk-telephone standing at one end of the library table. I wheeled and strode toward it.

"Wait—wait—you may be mistaken," whispered the woman, as she watched me reach for the receiver.

"That I intend to find out from the police," I retorted. "I have given you both a chance, and you insist on not taking it. Now I'm going to have an officer in this house as soon as one can get here!"

"An officer?"

"Yes, an officer! And I'm going to get to the bottom of this affair if it takes me a year!"

"You don't know what you're doing!" cried the terrified woman, coming toward me. She was shaking now, and wringing her hands.

"Perfectly," I responded, raising the receiver to my ear. I could hear her panting over me as I spoke into the transmitter. "Give me 3100 Spring, please. Give me police headquarters, quickly."

I almost forgot that I was acting a part. I almost failed to remember that I had more to fear from the office at the other end of the line than had the frightened woman who tried to drag me away from the transmitter. But I had not forgotten that familiar old trick of holding down the receiver-hook with my left hand. My message, of course, had never even reached the wire. Yet again I most heartily wished that my record had been clean, so that I might have pushed the thing to that bitterest end I had looked for. But already my threat had struck home.

"Wait, only wait," gasped the woman over me, "and I will explain everything."

"Everything, openly and honestly?" I demanded, still at the 'phone.

"Everything," she acquiesced, weakly.

I went through my pretence of cancelling the 'phone order and hung up the receiver. Then I turned to her. She sank into one of the wide-armed library chairs and covered her face with her hands. And she sat that way for several seconds, motionless, breathing heavily.

VIII

Her first words, when she spoke, were not to me, nor to any one in that room of shadow and silence.

"The poor girl!" she cried pityingly, with a note in her voice that made me feel small and puny and uncomfortable. "The poor girl!" She was not thinking of me, of what I might be or had been, but of the woman she had stood so ready to shield and save.

"Why can't you trust me?" I demanded.

She drew herself together slowly, and turned to me with what seemed a complete change of manner. Her face looked old and careworn and anxious in the broken light that came from the burning logs.

"I *can* trust you," she answered, a little bitterly, "for the simple reason that I am compelled to!"

"Then please explain."

"But you are not a physician—how can I?"

"That need not count."

"But you know nothing of this—of abnormal psychology."

"On the contrary, I am keenly interested in such things."

"You? In what way?"

"I have studied the psychology of crime for many years, and from many very diverse stand-points."

We looked at each other, silently. My solemnity seemed to convince her, but still she hesitated.

"This isn't altogether psychology," she amended.

14

"Perhaps not; but I am equally interested in psychic anæsthesia. I know something of Binet's *Felida X.*, for instance, and of Prince's *Beauchamp* case. And some day I intend to supply James with a foot-note for his study of *Mary Reynolds*!"

The nurse looked at me with a touch of wonder on her anxious face. She turned away to the fire, and continued to look at the flame as she went on.

"Then you know that amnesia doesn't always depend on esphlasis; that beyond the morbid forgetfulness of mere aphasia there can be an actual disintegrated personality."

"But what of that?"

"Simply this," she answered. "The woman you saw come into this house is a woman with a dual personality."

IX

"What, in this case, does that mean?"

"It means that this young woman is a mental neurotic—that she is one person with a terribly contradictory character; that at one time she is a gentle and beautiful girl, and at another a restless and irresponsible being who has to be watched like a child."

"Go on." A glimmer of light had at last come to me. With it, too, came an indeterminate sense of unrest. Consciousness, with me, had always seemed like a sea-traveller. When it anticipated and followed and dwelt on each roll and dip and plunge of its berth, it knew no sleep. But when it accepted the inevitable as natural and normal, and the conduct of the ship as the duty of some guarding captain on the bridge, then it relinquished the useless fight, and fell to sleep, even though that sleep were a broken and fitful one.

"I have been with her for four years now, since she first fell ill," the nurse was saying. "I come and go with her, from the country to the city. I went with her three times to Europe. I know her perfectly. And the more I see what she has to suffer the more my heart bleeds for her."

"What she has to suffer?" I echoed.

"Yes, suffer; for her case is hopeless. Janet, of Paris, thought it was only hysteria, but could do nothing. The neurologist who used to come once a week from Philadelphia on the case claimed that it was simply the mental side of her neurosis assuming the form of criminal psychosis. Schaumer agreed with him, in a way, and even attempted a cure by hypnotic suggestion. But there was no neuropathic heredity, and no actual hysterical epilepsy; so he failed. He couldn't even uncover the trauma that had first engendered the cleft. The Vienna specialist, who also treated it as a case of disintegrated personality, said it was like a wire burning out between two stations, under some sudden and too heavy current. It left the two parts of her unconnected, unco-ordinated. Something in her character seemed to have dissolved away."

"But has nothing been done?"

"Bromig, the Berlin alienist, said it was like water an electric current had passed through. It had divided into a hydrogen of moral responsibility, he said, and an oxygen of insanity. He said he had known of cases where some sudden explosion, as it were, had reunited the two gases and made them into water once more. He suggested restraint and observation. But that always had the effect of making her violent. So he asked us how he could cure a disease when he didn't even know what it was, and at last gave up the case."

"Then why is this girl allowed at liberty, if she is a dangerous criminal?" I demanded.

"She is *not* dangerous. She is not a criminal. If she is left free she is perfectly happy. And until you came there has been only one mistake, only one terrible mistake. They all had the Tiffany trade-stamp and a scratch number on, and we got them away from her at last and sent them back."

I could see her little shudder of horror at the memory of it.

"It has always been nothing more than a poor little childish eccentricity, a harmless and innocent whim in hiding things away."

"But what is at the root of it all? When and how did it begin?"

The woman walked softly to the locked door and listened for a moment before she started to speak again. She was now less ill at ease; her note was more intimate.

"It began four years ago, very mysteriously, yet very simply. It was a week after her father's death. I was first called in to take care of her that week. She was ill and worn out with suffering. It was at the old family home on lower Fifth Avenue. The place was broken into by a burglar. He forced an entrance through this girl's bedroom window, by climbing up some vines and cutting out a pane of glass. She heard him and switched on the lights. I needn't tell you what a terrible moment it was for her. The burglar in some way escaped. But the girl did not; she was already worn out and nervous. The shock left her sleepless and hysterical. We noticed nothing wrong, though, except that she drank three cups of black coffee at daybreak, put on her riding-habit, and had a horse saddled that had been shut up in the stables for two weeks."

I watched her as she paused; I was following every word.

"The horse ran away and threw her. She was unhurt, we all thought, except for the slightest injury to one of the carpal bones in her right hand. There was no blow on the head, no wound, no skull depression. But from that moment the trouble began."

"It all came, then, from an untimely shock to a weakened and especially vulnerable organization—a sort of violent convulsion of the mind, like a sudden paralytic stroke?"

"No, it was not altogether sudden. We noticed it first by her fretting over the little fracture to the carpal bone, even after it had healed and was perfectly well. Then the hysterical obsession, or, rather, the duality of personality, slowly began to show itself."

"One moment. Did it date from the burglary or from the hurt to the wrist bone?" I asked.

"From the burglary, I think, though it passed unnoticed at the time. We suspected nothing then, you see. Even her childish habit of picking things up and carrying them away and hiding them did not worry us at first. But as this line of division in all her temper and taste showed itself more and more, and the duality of character was actually noticeable, the habit grew stronger. It became a sort of mania, especially when what you would call her lower self was in control of her actions."

"Then is it all due to some association of ideas springing from her fright at the burglar?"

"Perhaps—but no one is sure of that. Indeed, they're sure of nothing."

"But you remember the *Hélène Smith* case, how Flournoy speaks of the dog and the priest who rescued her after her great fright? You remember how so many of her dream-men kept coming to her in priest's clothes?"

"I know; but none of this has ever cleared up the poor child's mystery," was the nurse's half-bitter, half-weary retort.

"But can't she explain, herself? Doesn't she remember things afterward?"

"Only vaguely. She has no sense of shame even—but you must bear in mind that she's never wicked or evil at heart. I could never have stayed with her so long if she had been *that*. It's only that she can't see the difference between good and bad when this break in personality comes on. It simply leaves her unmoral, the same as a child is unmoral."

I had not yet reached a solution of the point that most puzzled me. There were reasons, strange reasons I could not altogether explain, why this case so held my interest. It seemed like a story I had listened to, long ago,—a story I had listened to, and fallen asleep in the hearing.

"But is there no physical taint as well?" I asked. "I mean, is she sane and well in body?"

I waited for some betraying glance of fear, for some significant start. But there was none.

"I don't understand," said the puzzled woman.

"Is there no actual malformation of flesh and bone, no abnormal feature of—of limb?"

"None; I'm sure," was her response.

"Are you *certain*?" I persisted.

"Quite certain," she answered, looking at me in wonder. "The only thing at all like that was the foolish little delusion that came with the injury to the carpal bone in her right hand. But I've already told you of that."

"*That* may be it!" I cried. "Please explain it a little more."

"She sometimes thinks this arm is dead."

"Dead?" I echoed.

"Yes; she nursed the idea, at times, that her right hand was useless. I always thought it was because of the splints and having it so tightly dressed when she was hysterical and sick, that the pain may have left a morbid impression on her mind."

She paused meditatively, and I hung forward for her next words. As I did so the silence of the unlighted room was pierced by the sound of a sharp cry from above. It was a woman's voice, shrill and imperious, calling.

"Miss Shattuck!" Then a silence. "Jeffreys!" Then more loudly and with a rising note of alarm, "Miss Shattuck!"

X

The nurse started up in dismay and ran to the door. She motioned for me to stay back as she opened it. The hallway itself was unlighted. So I followed her out, at a venture.

The woman was calling from the head of the stairs. I could just make out the black mass of her figure in the dim light from an open doorway to the left.

"*Who is in this house?*" called the shrill voice above.

"What is it?" asked the nurse temporizingly, as she motioned me back into the deeper gloom toward the vestibule.

"Who is in this house?" demanded the woman at the head of the stairs, the note of authority high above that of alarm.

"It's the man from the Edison Company to inspect the wiring," I whispered into the nurse's ear. I found myself clutching her tight by the arm.

"It's a wire inspector from the Edison Company," answered the nurse. I could hear the street-noises in the silence that followed. I stepped softly back and closed the inner vestibule door, for a chance opening of the outer portal might at any moment betray my presence there. Carefully as I closed that door, it broke the dead silence of the listening house.

"Did he go?" asked the girl, hearing the sound.

"Yes," I whispered. "Say 'Yes.'"

"He has just gone," answered the nurse.

"Then tell Jeffreys to lock up, please, and to see to the lights," she called down, more easily.

I backed away quickly as she spoke, backed into the remotest corner of the hall. For the woman at the stairhead had suddenly lifted a hand and switched on the electrolier that rose from the high carved figure of a water nymph rising out of the baluster beside her.

I could see her then, as distinctly as though she had been bathed in sunlight. Her hat was off, but she still wore her coat and the black lynx boa over her shoulders. I could see the Roman braid of deep chestnut, the pale ivory of the still girlish face, the thin yet well-poised body, the birdlike side movements of the head, the childish wilfulness of the half-pouting lips, very red, and drooping a little at the corners.

"You must go—oh, please go!" whispered the nurse through the darkness. But I stood there without moving, watching the figure above.

For the girl had slipped down to the floor on the landing, crooning like a child. She threw back one end of the boa, and I noticed the quick, restless motion or two of her left hand.

Then, for a moment or two, she studied the gloved fingers of her right hand, pressing them back and forth idly, and all the while singing quietly to herself. Yet, when she looked up, her eyes had the vague indirection of stare that one sees in a sleep-walker.

Then, with a quick little laugh, she raised the gloved hand up before her staring eyes. *It came away from her body without a sound; it swung free, like the limb of a broken doll.*

XI

An audible gasp broke from my lips, a gasp of wonder and horror.

The girl herself must have heard it, for she started to her feet with a child-like little scream. As she did so the arm fell from her fingers, spindled forward to the step-edge, balanced there a moment, and then came tumbling and falling down the bare wooden stairway, step by step, rolling out almost to my feet.

It was a gloved thing of steel and wood, a jointed and buckled mechanism as insensate as the boards across which it lay.

"See, see! There goes my Other Self!" cried the girl, shrilly, crazily, as she watched that rolling and horrible limb. There seemed something comic in its movement to her, something wild and ridiculous, for she burst into a sudden peal of laughter. It was the laughter that leads to hysteria, to delirium, and in a moment she was sobbing and crying insanely, "My Other Self! My Other Self!" and the nurse was almost dragging me toward the street door.

"You *must* go. You must leave this house," she commanded, with a desperate low note of authority, of finality, that left me a little afraid of her.

"But I can't go now. You forget what I came for."

"Can't you see it's useless—now? That it's worse than cruel?"

"Yes; but still I can't go."

"I tell you, you *must*!"

She drew away from me in the gloom, and I heard the pregnant, metallic movement of a door-lock.

"Leave this house!" she almost screamed. I felt no twinge of pity before the tragedy of her tortured voice, for I followed a calling on which Sentiment always rode clumsily. But I drew back involuntarily before her sudden, fierce onslaught. And before I had quite realised it she had thrust me far enough through the open door to slam and lock and bolt it in my face.

I contemplated it, a little angrily, a little threateningly. Then, I think, I laughed out loud, almost glad of the cool night air that blew on my face, beaded with sweat. I had met with defeat, but I could still return to the field.

XII

It was precisely twenty minutes past two, in the dead of night, that I returned. Just what reaction of feeling took me back I no longer tarried to understand. Yet I knew it was not so much the quest of what was rightfully my own as the sting of frustration under which I had last crept away from that quiet and unbetraying mask of graystone behind which such unexpected things had been said and done. More than ever, at this new shift of things, I wanted to see the end of the game for game's sake.

My avenue of approach was a discreetly indirect one, and carefully watching my chance I tried the basement doors of three different apartment-houses on Riverside Drive. The lock of the third one was suited to my keys, so I let myself in, and crept along the entire length of the asphalted corridor, past dumb-waiter and elevator shafts, a furnace and engine room, ash-barrels and whitewashed walls, to the rear of the building, where a door barred my way out. The mere sliding of a bolt, however, brought me freedom. I found myself in a little court crossed and recrossed by pulley-lines and backed by a high board fence.

I scrambled over this fence as noiselessly as possible. My one fear at this juncture was dogs—those nervous, over-pampered, light-sleeping dogs of the well-to-do. The house I wanted was still two courts to the south, so I had still two more high board fences, one of them surmounted by an espalier of barb-wire. This wire I cut with my pocket pliers. Then I slipped on my face-mask, made from

21

the back of an old glove: I did not care to be recognised in the house before me.

Nor was it an inviting place, I found, after I had dropped quietly into the court and spent a minute or two in studious inspection of its vine-covered back wall. Every window on the first and second floors was heavily barred. The door itself was impregnable. And from the number of wires I saw leading out into space, faintly visible in the clear starlight, I realised that the place was equipped with a complete nervous-system of signal-circuits, that the slightest contact with any one of them would be my irreparable undoing.

Groping about the court I found two empty dog-kennels. These, put on end against the wall, made it possible for me to get a footing in the loops of the wistaria branches, the lower main-stalks being carefully boxed and spiked. I worked upward and outward toward the southern corner of the house, where the vines ran into a framework studded with insulators.

I carried no wire with me, so my first task was to find enough metal for a "jumper." This I audaciously cut out of what looked to be a telephone circuit. Then I climbed still higher, until I reached what was either a Holmes or a Metropolitan Protective line. Being a burglar-alarm system, I had every reason to suspect it would be operated on a "closed circuit." So I settled back into a more secure foothold on the vines, and carefully scraped the insulation-tissue from a portion of the wires before me. Then I just as carefully ran my "jumper" between these two bald spots, cutting out and "killing" the window-area above me, very much as a placer-miner might dam back and divert a stream that threatened some newer field of operations. Then I worked my way carefully upward, along the swaying vines, sometimes slipping and breaking through—sometimes, as the growth became more tenuous, finding it next to impossible to get a footing.

XIII

The city was very quiet. Only now and then the whistle of a river-boat tore a hole in the silence. I was hot and breathing hard by the time I reached the third-story window. It was, in fact, two windows, side by side, with only a graystone column between them. Set in the glass pane of one was a brass ventilator, spinning slowly with its suction of air. I tried this window and then the next. Both were securely locked. I worked my way higher, and at last got a footing on the broad sill. The blinds were drawn; there was no sign of life within. Then I quietly and methodically proceeded to follow what would be 'Frisco Slim's plan of campaign in such cases.

I first glued my spare piece of glove-back to the upper pane, just above the sash fastening, leaving it there to harden while I worked. Then I took out my glass-cutter (it was merely a diamond chip sunk in a piece of steel) and slowly drew a half moon on the pane, just above the sash cross-bar.

Then I crouched there waiting and listening, for my next move could not be made without its fitting accompaniment. That accompaniment came with the muffling sound of a prolonged ferry-whistle from the Hudson. As it boomed out through the night I struck the half-moon a sharp blow with the steel of my glass-cutter. The crack, following the line of least resistance, fell directly along the diamond scratch.

I pulled gently outward on the bit of glued glove-back. As I did so the segment of glass came with it. Then I listened again before reaching in a carefully exploring hand. As I had expected, the burglar-alarm wires were there. I reached in and unlocked the sash, muffling the catch with my hand to deaden any possible sound. Then I slowly, cautiously, raised the window, inch by inch. A moment later I stood inside the room.

I waited there by the window, without a movement. During that wait both eye and ear and nostril were terribly alive and alert. I could even hear the quick, regular pump of my own heart.

I always hated operating above the first story. The house, too, was still a network of unknown wires; the jar of a door or the touch of a button might spell catastrophe. And all women, and especially all invalids, were notoriously unsettled and uncertain sleepers.

There was neither light nor sound in the room where I stood. But something warned me that the room was a bedroom, and that it was occupied. I knew this instinctively, in the same way, I suppose, that a wild animal can sniff life far down the wind.

It caused me to drop low, on my hands and knees, as I moved forward. But still I heard no sound beyond the occasional gentle creaking of my own knee-cap. My outstretched fingers came in contact with heavy, cool metal highly polished. I felt it cautiously, inch by inch. It was the burnished brass rods of a bed. I was at the foot of it, for I could feel a coverlet between the heavy rods.

XIV

I rose to my feet slowly, until I stood upright. As I did so I was struck lightly on the coat-sleeve by something—by a mysterious something that sent a tingle of terror up and down my backbone. I threw up a hand instinctively, for I knew that moving Thing, whatever it was, had not been touched or liberated by me. Again I felt it; and this time I caught at it with my frenzied fingers, clutching it with strained attention.

Then a second tingle of apprehension went through me. For the thing that had swung out toward me was the wooden drop-button of an electric light, swaying on its insulated cords from the ceiling above the bed.

What stung me into sudden alertness was the fact that some hand other than mine had started its movement. Somebody on the bed before me had held and released it. Somebody facing me had thought to turn on the light, but through fear, or cunning, or weakness had not done so! There was danger, imminent danger, there before me, confronting me.

I dropped my right hand with the quickness of thought, and drew my short-barreled yegger's revolver. The bed might be already empty. There was no sound, no movement. Perhaps I was already trapped.

On calmer second thoughts I knew no one could have slipped from that bed without my knowing or hearing it. Whatever was awaiting me or threatening me was still there on the bed.

I brought my right arm down and forward, leaning low over the brass foot-rail, as far forward as I could reach. Once sure my revolver covered the head of the bed, I cocked the trigger. The snap of the spring sounded like an explosion. Then the thumb of my upraised left hand, which still clung to the little wooden bulb on the wire-end, pushed upward on the compressible button.

The movement flooded the room with light—blinding white light, that left sense dazed for a second of uncertainty. Then the scene that lay before my eyes suddenly flashed back and registered

24

in the camera of consciousness. It left there a picture as minute and vivid and indelible as a photographic impression.

XV

In the wide, white bed before me, within three feet of me, half-sat, half-huddled the woman of the third arm. Her eyes were wide and staring. The skin of her face and neck looked blue-white, and I could see the blue veins at her throat and temples. Her lips were parted and colourless, and her lower jaw had fallen away a little, so that as her bosom suddenly began to pump up and down I could distinctly hear the short, quick breath wheeze through her parted teeth.

Never before, in all my days, had I beheld such terror, such inarticulate and motionless and impotent terror, as she wheezed and panted there, staring past the barrel of my menacing revolver to my own black-masked face above her at the foot of the bed.

The blue-white of her eyeballs never varied, never moved. But a slow convulsive tremor shook her huddled body. She seemed to draw and shiver up into a mummylike mockery of herself. She seemed to crumple and warp together by the contraction of all the cords in her fragile body. As she did so, I caught sight of a pigskin wallet clutched crazily in her fingers. It was my own—the wallet that held my stolen money.

I bent forward and tore it from her unresisting clutch with one sweep of my left arm. As I did this, one tortured, involuntary scream of abject terror burst on my ears. With a galvanic movement, as quick as the snap of a released watch-spring, the woman's over-tensioned frame rebounded and fell backward over the edge of the bed.

Some shadow of that terror leaped to my own heart. I sprang for the window. Even before I had it open I heard the sound of voices and running footsteps. So I swung out, clinging to the vines, on one side of the sill, not daring to move.

As I clung there, flat against the wall, I could hear the cries of alarm in the bedroom, the sounds on the floor as the girl was lifted back to the bed, the hurried calls and orders, the distant tinkle of a bell. Then I heard the voice of the nurse, coaxing, soothing, reassuring, and above it suddenly the second great cry of the girl.

It was like the cry of the sleeper awakened:

"*Oh, my head—my head!*" It was the voice of reason, of sanity, of release. "*It's—it's different! It's all come back! My arm's alive again!*"

I half-slid, half-scrambled down the vines, though as I did so I could hear the quiet but happy sobbing of the woman on the bed. The soul-cleft had re-adjusted itself! *The explosion had reunited the gases!*

CHAPTER TWO
THE ADVENTURE OF THE UNKNOWN DOOR

I

A city can seem very small, when you are not quite sure which quarter of it is harbouring an enemy. Yet I kept telling myself that I ought to feel safe enough there, in the noise and crowd of Broadway. For it was high noon, when the cavedwellers who labour above the cañon descended for an hour to eat and then swarmed back to work. I kept dipping into that crowd of honest toilers, deeper and deeper, like a chased dabchick, letting it carry me along, and breathing freer every minute. My suit-case, weighed down with my newly acquired Outfit, was rather heavy, it is true. But I swung it freely, as though it held nothing more than a hair-brush and a change of linen.

Then I came to a standstill and backed water, quickly. For lounging aimlessly against the street-corner news-stand was Doogan's plain-clothes man, MacKisknie. His hands were in his pockets and a cheroot dropped languidly from one corner of his mouth. His eyes were half shut and sleepy-looking. But those half-shut eyes were watching every face that passed up and down the east side of Broadway. Every atom of that human tide which ebbed and flowed about him had to pass muster in the alert brain behind those sleepy-looking eyes. The entire street had to seep through that sentinel consciousness, like turbid water through a filter.

I swung round sharply and shouldered my way out, straight east into one of the side streets. It left me unscreened and in the open, but it was the only thing to do. Once east to Park Avenue, and north to Forty-second Street and I could catch any out-going train from the Grand Central.

A patter of rain came down from the blackening sky and freckled the dusty asphalt. I wanted to rest the arm that carried the suit-case. It began to ache by this time with the weight of the Outfit. So I put it down on a house-step beside me, on the pretext of turning up my trousers. I was still stooping when my glance travelled eastward, and fell on a slowly approaching figure.

27

I continued to stoop, for it was a Seventeenth Precinct patrolman. And since the Canfield case, I had no love for patrolmen of that particular precinct, nor they for me. There was no time for the weighing of alternatives, for quibbling about methods. I had to act, and act quickly. So I simply caught up my suit-case and went briskly up the steps that stood before me.

They were brownstone steps, wide and deep and ponderous, and they led to what seemed an equally ponderous brownstone house. An electric bell glimmered from beside the high, gloomy-looking doors.

I made a pretence of pushing the button, with my heart in my mouth. My first hope was that the house would be empty. It looked deserted enough from the street. I tried to think of a name to ask for; but nothing reasonable came to my mind. Then I pushed the button in earnest, for the passing steps were now directly beneath me, and half-measures were dangerous.

The door opened instantly, as though the figure had been waiting there for some call other than mine. It flashed through my mind that I might have pushed the button that first time, after all.

I noticed, as the door swung back slowly and ponderously, like the great gate of a canal-lock, that it was apparently of solid mahogany. I next noticed that the figure just inside the open door was arrayed in the green livery-cloth of a footman, with four metal buttons on each side of the long-tailed service-coat. I would have bolted on the instant, but it was too late for the man in front of me, and too early for the man behind.

I looked at the footman a little closer as the door opened its widest. He seemed gazing out at me with dead eyes, cold, impassive, unconcerned, yet with something watching and alert about them. The man's face was coarse in feature, the skin flaccid and colourless, the mouth hard and cruel.

"Does Mr. Gahan live here?" I demanded.

"He does, sir," came the answer, quick as an echo.

"Mr. Edward Elton Gahan?"

"Yes, sir."

I peered in at the man. *Edward Elton Gahan was my own name.*

II

"Is Mr. Gahan at home?" I asked, more casually, steadying myself.

"I think so, sir." Something about the man made me afraid of him.

"Er—shall I call again?" I suggested.

"He's expecting you, sir," was the reply, obsequiously yet, it seemed to me, half-mockingly made. The man in livery stepped back, making way for me. I didn't dare look around to satisfy myself that the steps on the sidewalk below had passed on. It was too late to hesitate. I had to see the thing through.

It was raining gently but steadily down in the street. I stepped into the darkened hallway with my suit-case still in my hand. The ponderous door swung slowly to, and closed behind me with a metallic click of its latch.

"This way, sir," said the dead-eyed footman, leading up the wide stairway of polished hardwood.

I went after him, reluctantly, cautiously, feeling that I was being sucked against my own will deeper and deeper into some black whirlpool. At the head of the stairs, the footman in green turned to the right, toward what was the front of the house. Each door we passed was closed. But what I could see of the halls gave me the impression of a solidly furnished Knickerbocker house of fifty years ago.

I had no time for further thought. The footman was already knocking at the door confronting us. A feeble and querulous voice said "Come in," and a moment later I had passed under another lintel into another room.

Before me, in a high-backed invalid's chair, sat a man of about forty. He wore a huge, quilted dressing-gown, and the lower part of his body was covered by what seemed a woollen shawl. His hands were long and thin and tremulous, and I could detect the bas-relief blue veining on the back of them. His shoulders, once massive and wide, now seemed drawn in and stooped. I caught a glimpse of the bony protuberance of his Adam's-apple in the lean and hawk-like neck. The lines of the thin face seemed almost quadrangular, with the short, square jaw, and the high white forehead. The hair was scant and grayish. But what most impressed me was the colourlessness of the face, as I swept that man who bore my own name with one quick and searching glance.

"This is the gentleman to see you, sir," said the footman. I seemed to catch a touch of mockery in his deferential tone, just as I had been vaguely disconcerted at first by the pregnant yet placid indifference of his eyes. It seemed the unconcern of a man who knew something and yet chose to remain silent. There was almost pity in his servile condescension, something muffled and fateful. And it put me more and more on my guard.

The man in the invalid's chair peered up at me, a little startled, I think. He studied me for a minute of unbroken silence. There suddenly seemed something sepulchral and tomb-like in the quietness of that gloomy house.

I looked for some change of face, some shock of surprise, in the big-framed invalid. But he gave no sign. His deep-sunk, ratlike, little eyes bowed into me without the alteration of one line in the pallid mask of a face in which they were set. They made me uncomfortable. I began to wonder how I could lie out of my dilemma. Then I began to wonder what strange happenings could make it needful that I should be lured quietly in through that gloomy door. The familiar and intoxicating sense of something impending seemed to float about me.

For the first time I let my eyes wander from the great figure in the high-backed chair, and discovered that we were not alone in the room. In the half-shadow between the two high windows that faced the north stood yet another figure. It was that of a man about my own age, thick-set, stockily built, with a dark face, deep-lined and predaceous. He stood with his arms folded, backed against the wall. And his attitude seemed one of waiting. But he, too, was silent.

All this was revealed to me in one quick glance, as I let my gaze coast the great high-ceilinged room. Then I looked back at the figure in the invalid's chair.

"What was the name, Dickson?" he asked, complainingly, half-turning to the immovable footman in green. His voice was querulous, almost a whine. Yet it carried a hidden menace, a reproof, as much as to say: "You fool, you'll smart for this!"

"My name is Gahan," I cut in.

I waited for some start of surprise. But there was none. The name left him unmoved. I turned quickly to the servant, my suspicions verified. He stood there motionless, inert, unbetraying.

The invalid made an impatient movement of the hand. It was directed toward the man who stood waiting between the two windows. He crossed the room, in answer to the sign, and opened a door in the south wall. As the door opened, and he stepped through, the busy pound and clatter of a telegraph relay broke on my ears. I tried to catch some inkling of its message, some hint of the Morse. But the period between the opening and the closing of the door had been too brief.

III

The sound seemed to electrify the invalid into sudden and unlooked-for strength. He turned on me impatiently.

"What's your business?" he demanded. A moment before I was ready to explain my presence as solely due to a mistaken house number. Something in the sound of the clattering relay, however, had already challenged my curiosity. I decided to give my friend in the invalid's chair a dose of his own medicine.

"You knew *that* when you sent for me," I evaded, with the utmost solemnity.

The invalid flashed a sudden look of warning at me. It was the first unguarded moment. If I was still in the dark, so was he. But toward what was I stumbling and groping? What was taking place behind those closed and mysterious doors?

"Umph—of course!" temporised the other, nervously. I could see the wheels of thought hard at work behind that immobile mask.

"Dickson!" he cried out, suddenly, "be so good as to take the gentleman's bag."

I fell back a step or two, guardedly.

"It's no trouble," I protested, equably, though I could feel my body moisten and prickle with a nervous perspiration. Again the ratlike eyes studied my face. I felt that he was deliberating over me as a terrier deliberates over a cornered victim before its *coup de grâce*.

The silence was broken by the door of the back room being flung open. It was blocked by the square-set man. He appeared nervous and excited.

"We've got it, sir," he called out, triumphantly. "We've got it—it's going through at last!"

If wishes were daggers that man in the door would never have made another such announcement on earth, I take it, from the flash of the invalid's little eyes. But I paid no attention to this, for through the open door there still again crept into my ears the businesslike clatter of the sounder. Involuntarily I stood there, coercing attention.

My attitude must have betrayed me, for the man in the invalid's chair suddenly sprang to his feet. I saw for the first time that his leg was bandaged. I also saw that there was six feet and more of him, and that he was far less fragile than he had appeared.

"Dickson!" he cried, sharply—and there was no tremulousness in his voice this time—"let this man out, at once!"

Our eyes met, and he knew I understood. He had read the look of latent combativeness on my face at that peremptory dismissal. I laughed, I don't know why, but I laughed aloud. Perhaps it was at the wholeheartedness of his decision, the audacity of his challenge; perhaps it was relief at finding something against which to focus my suspicion.

"Wait!" cried the invalid, in rapid afterthought. "This is the man to test the meters, Dickson. Show him down to the basement by way of the front door. Then let him in by way of the area, *if he wishes*."

The placid cut-throat in green livery again held the door for me, and again I laughed. But, as I stepped out of that strange room, I could see the invalid stalk to the inner door, and dart through to the chamber in the rear, whence came the clicking of the telegraph relay. A moment later, I was in the hallway, following the imperturbable Dickson down the polished steps.

IV

As I followed the man in green livery through the quiet house, I decided on my plan of action. Something about the line of his right hip had keenly interested me, and I knew that anything I did must be done both guardedly and thoroughly.

Between the inner and outer doors of the main entrance was the vestibule. It was probably six feet by ten in size, walled in right and left, and barred back and front by the ponderous hardwood doors.

I dropped my bag at the precise moment that the man in livery stooped to unlock the outer door. Before that bag struck the floor, my right knee was in the small of his back, and I had given him the "Calgary Crook." He crumpled down under it, with a little groan of pain, twisting half-way around. I fell on him as he collapsed, with both knees on his chest. His breath went from his lungs, at the impact, with a ludicrous grunt.

Then, first of all, I carefully removed the revolver which had broken the regular line of his right hip. Then I unhooked his ring of house-keys. Then, before the breath could come back to his lungs, I locked the outer door and withdrew the key. Catching up my bag, I closed and locked the second door, and left him there a prisoner. Then I waited a moment or two to recover my own breath, and decide what the next move should be. I felt more at home with a revolver once more in my side-pocket. I would feel still more at home, I knew, once a second door had been found in case of emergency.

Straight before me, at the south end of the dark hall, another door stood.

I tried it and found it locked. The fourth key fitted.

When I entered, I entered guardedly, with my hand in my right coat-pocket. My first impression was that the room was empty. My second was that the windows were barred and grated like the windows of a mediæval dungeon. Then I discovered that I was not alone in the room.

Standing at one of the windows with her back to me was a woman. She wore a hat, a black-plumed hat, and a loose-fitting cravenette street-coat. Even from where I stood, I could see two things—that she was a young woman, and that she had a great deal of dark brown hair. She did not turn as I quickly locked the door, and advanced into the room. There seemed something defiant in the line of her shoulders.

"Madam!" I said, sharply, for time was very precious.

She did not move, and I repeated the call, hurrying toward her.

She wheeled about, slowly, disdainfully, and swept me with one single glance of scorn and loathing. For the first time, I took my right hand out of my pocket—*that*, at least, was needless.

"Who are you?" I cried, nettled by her look.

I saw for the first time, too, that she was really shaking and quivering; whether with fear, or indignation, or both, I could not tell. I also saw that she was different from most other women I had ever spoken to. She was in some way even different from those groups of girls I had so often seen in front of the Twenty-third Street and the Fifth Avenue shops and about the Broadway theatres and candy-stores—those fast-talking, loud-laughing, well-groomed girls, blonde and fresh in colour, weighed down with furs and crowned with enormous hats. She seemed to have their vitality, their poise, their smoothness of skin. But she had something else; some colder and older and more resolute bearing, something that made her face a woman's even while her figure was still a girl's.

"Who are you?" I repeated.

"You will realise who I am, and I think you will realise it bitterly, once I am out of this house, and you are called to account for such an outrage—such an insult—such a crime."

She spoke slowly and her voice shook with passion.

"What have I done?"

"Done! You have done what a Sicilian brigand wouldn't dare to do. *You have kept me a prisoner in this house and this room for three hours.*"

V

"Kept you a prisoner!" I echoed, foolishly. I fell back amazed, bewildered by the complications of the currents that eddied and tangled about me.

My face wore such a look of wonder that the girl took a step or two toward me, and suddenly cried out, with a new ring of life and hope in her voice: "Who are *you*?"

"Listen!" I cried. "I haven't been in this house half an hour. I have never been in it before to-day. I stand as much a prisoner here as you do. I'm in danger, too, if this house is one of danger."

"It is!" she broke in.

"But *how?*—*how?* I can't understand it. I can't make out what it all means. For the love of Heaven, if you know, tell me, and tell me quickly!"

Suddenly, without warning, her shoulders began to heave and shake. I don't know what it was, but for one precious minute she turned away and cried into her handkerchief, silently. I watched her for a moment, then I ran to the door and listened. Any sound might bring some new turn to that mysterious drama.

"We're losing time," I said, brusquely. The sight of her tears made me a little uncomfortable.

She looked up at me closely, atoningly, with a sudden gasp of relief.

"Are you a detective?" she asked. I might have lied, but I was afraid of the honest candour of her eyes.

"I am not, I am sorry to say," was my calm reply.

"Then what are you?" she demanded, with a return of suspicion.

"That's neither here nor there," I evaded. "But this point is clear: I've no friend inside this house. But if you're in trouble here, and want help, I'm here to help you."

She still studied my face, piqued, I think, by the impersonality of my feelings. I began to see that she was a young woman who in her own more rose-grown walk of life instinctively and openly engaged the affections of those about her, relying on the soft appeal of sex, as a rule, for the accomplishment of her ends. But, oddly enough, I grew hot under her gaze, though my very embarrassment seemed to reassure her.

"I shall see that you are paid, well paid," she protested. Her reference to pay enraged me. Again she reminded me of the petted house-dog confronted by the feral laws of the open.

"That's rubbish! I've already told you I'm no detective. And we're wasting time, good time. Every second counts. Now explain quick, as well as you can."

"I can't explain," she retorted, hurriedly, "any more than you can."

"But you *must*, at once, if we're to get out of here."

"All that I can tell you is, my father has been busy and worried and sick—the last few days I've been helping him."

"Pardon me, but who is your father?"

She surveyed me with the indignation of a celebrity held up for passports. She hadn't been in the habit, plainly, of enlarging on who and what she was.

"Father's name is Shaler. You may know him as the President of the Mexican East Coast and director of the Michiocan and Campeche Railway. He's also the head of the City International Bank, and one of the owners of the Gulf and Yucatán Railway."

I noticed, for the first time, some imp of comedy playing about her lips, as she finished her recital of offices.

"Is that enough?" she demanded.

"Quite enough," was my answer.

She turned and looked at me again, perplexed, apparently, by my expression.

"Have you a brother?" I asked, to explain my look of wonder.

Her eyes were both searching and suspicious, as she suddenly demanded: "Do *you* know *him*?" But they were very beautiful eyes.

"No, I don't," I answered, and this was true (for it was only the name that was familiar to me). "But I want to know more about your father. What were you saying about his work?"

"I was going to say that it was my father who engineered the Mexican half of the Pan-American System. That's what has worried him so these last few weeks. It's such an important amalgamation plan and stock merger that a woman reporter offered our home operator two thousand dollars for news about it. You see, everything has to be done secretly, or Wall Street speculators would take advantage of any leak, and exploit the movement, and hurt father's prestige. So we had a private wire run into the study at home, and a woman operator has been coming every afternoon and staying until seven."

"Where is your home?"

"Seven doors east of this house."

"Go on."

"All I know is that the merger was to be effected to-day, but they're having trouble in Washington, and Senator Hewlitt, who acts for father, has been keeping the wire busy all afternoon. As soon as father and his secretary get up from downtown he keeps sending messages out and getting replies. He told me last night that to-day would probably be his Waterloo. That's what makes me know this all means some evil to him."

"What started it?"

"First there was a newspaper woman trying to bribe our operator. Then a trained nurse came to the house this morning. There seemed to be nothing wrong about that, for it turned out she had merely made a mistake in the house number. But for some reason, I watched her. She hurried on to this house and that made me suspicious. Then later in the day, a telephone inspector came. That made me more suspicious. I kept him waiting until I could 'phone down to the company's office. They knew of no one who had been sent. So I ran upstairs and there I found him prowling about the study. I was frightened then, and hurried back to the 'phone and called up the police station. Before I could drop the receiver he ran downstairs and was outside. I followed him, for I thought at first that he might have stolen something. He came here, to this house, just as the nurse did. I rang the bell, thinking only of not losing him. I was so excited and indignant I scarcely thought at all. Then, before I quite realised it, I was here, in this room, a prisoner."

VI

I saw everything at a glance—the busy sounder upstairs, the tapped wire and the preliminary messages being read, the readily opened door, and the movement to entrap and hold a sufficiently suspicious stranger before he could interfere, the conspirators awaiting the final despatch, the accomplices who would plunge the limit on the new Mexican merger, the thousands on thousands of dollars of illicit and unearned gains, the stubborn bravery of the uncomprehending girl, the audacity and desperation of the whole carefully evolved scheme.

"Quick, where's your father now?" I demanded, without time even to explain. She caught up her little hunting-case watch.

"He's lunching at the Waldorf with the Western directors. Then he was to hurry home and talk with Senator Hewlitt over the wire. He asked the operator to be there before two."

"And what time does the Stock Exchange close?"

"At three."

"Then until three o'clock not a message, not a word, must go out of this house."

37

Dickson had not yet been missed, or a search would have been started, and some evidence of it would have come before us. That implied the other men were still held close, watching the wire, above stairs. I ran to the back window. There was nothing in the shape of a wire either visible or accessible from the ground floor.

"Does this mean any harm to father?" cried the girl.

"It means danger to us—until we get out of here!"

She came a little closer to me.

"But can you help him?" she pleaded.

"Tell me, first, does your private wire run in from the top of your house?"

She pondered a moment. "Yes, from the cornice; I remember that."

"Quick, then; we've got to get to the top of this house. I could leave you here, but it's safer—"

"I'd rather go with you," she said. We were no longer quite strangers.

I caught up my bag, ran to the door, and unlocked it, talking all the while.

"Listen. If we're to help your father and save his money and his good name, perhaps, you must do what I say, word for word. The wire that goes into your house passes from the Broadway cable galleries somewhere along the roof of this house. That wire has been tapped."

"Tapped?"

"Yes; tapped. Every message, every secret, going in and out of your father's study, can now be intercepted, listened to, and acted on."

We were on the stairs by this time, and I dropped my voice to a whisper.

"The only thing left for us to do is to cut every wire running into or over this house, at once. That stops their work, shuts them off. But as soon as that's done, they'll see the line is 'dead.' Then we'll have to scheme or fight our way out, the best we can. If not that, we must hold them off until the police come, or the Postal-Union sends a lineman to trace up the trouble."

"If I only knew he was safe," she whispered, pantingly, at the top of the first stairway. Her eyes were on me, searchingly, wonderingly. "Shhh!" I said, to hide the sudden feeling that swept through my veins at some new and foolish look of gratitude in her upturned face, white through the gloom of the shadowy hall.

Then I whispered "Wait," for through the quietness my ear had caught the muffled and hurried sound of voices shot through with the busy and metallic clicking of the telegraph key. We stood outside the door that led into the improvised operating room. I crept over to that door and pressed my ear flat against the panel, and leaned there listening. The girl stood beside me, intently watching my face. My suspicions had been correct.

VII

At the end of a wire in a quiet study not two hundred yards away was being consummated a movement which might some day change the complexion of maps, which was destined to make new cities and build unheard-of seaports, a movement which was to make into one system three thousand miles of wandering steel rails twining and glimmering across arid wastes, curling through narrow cañons and old Spanish villages, along sun-steeped valleys patrolled by swarthy and placid watchmen, little dreaming of the destinies being forged by one tiny brazen hammer, pounding on a piece of metal, so many miles away.

I could read the wire, but only brokenly. Yet it was enough to tell me that the movement was under way. The first orders and instructions were going through. I swung around to the waiting girl and pointed to the floor above.

"There are three floors. We must go to the top. Quick, and remember I am behind you, with a loaded revolver in my right hand, if anything happens. Quick, but no noise!"

"What does it mean?" she asked, with her eyes again on my face. But there was no time to explain.

"Your father's at home, safe," I whispered to her, at the head of the second stairway. "I just heard him speak—I mean, send out his orders—over the wire," I added, in answer to her look of wonder.

"Then they're stealing our news?"

"Every word of it," I answered.

We were now on the top floor. Before us stretched a hallway, narrower than that of the lower stories. It opened into what was once

39

a child's nursery or playroom, the walls brightly papered with fairy-lore figures. In the rear were three small windows, heavily barred.

I turned a key in the door, locking it. Then I flung up the middle window. The half-inch iron bars stood about eight inches apart. Planting my feet firmly against the sash, I pulled on the second bar. It bent a little, and that was all. I tried the next bar. It, too, bent with my weight, but scarcely three inches. Then I saw that the left end of the bar fitted loose in its socket. Pivoting it round and round, I finally worked it free, so that it slid in the side-pieces, slid until one end was at last released. With a quick twist, as with a lever, I bent the bar in, leaving an open passage.

Above my head, from the old-fashioned cornice, ran four wires. I could see, from the fresh wood showing through the scratched paint close beside an insulator-shank, that those wires had been recently strung. Those were the wires I had to kill.

The cornice hung two feet and more out over the walls. It was on the very edge of this cornice that the wires ran. My next problem was to reach them. For stretch as I might, with even the added inches of my lineman's pliers, the window-sill stood too far below. Under me, a sheer fall of fifty feet, was a spiked iron railing and the stone-paved courtyard. And valuable time was being lost, and vast things might be thrilling over those puny little strings of fate, not ten inches beyond my reach.

I turned and swept the room with my eyes. In one corner stood a narrow children's blackboard, screwed to the wall. It was made of half-inch pine, framed with oak, and must have been from eight to ten feet long. I sprang at it, insanely tore it from its fastenings, and leaned one end on the window-sill. Then I thrust it out into space. It should raise me the needed ten inches, if only so fragile a scaffolding would bear my weight.

I gave the girl my revolver. "You'll have to stand on this end of the board, see, to hold it down. It won't be hard—only remember, I am hanging fifty feet over a spiked railing. Quick!"

She shuddered a little. "Oh, be careful!" she gasped. I was already squirming and working my way out between the broken bars.

I tested the strength of my platform, cautiously. It seemed safe. Rising slowly, I touched the overhanging cornice with my left hand. A moment later, I had clutched at the tin eaves-troughing along the cornice-edge. It was raining in the world outside—I could feel the cool drops on my upturned face. Carefully balancing my weight, I raised the other hand with the lineman's pliers. The steel jaws bit into the metal; it swung lifeless from its insulator. Cautiously I cut the next wire and then the next. I could see little of the room within from where I hung. Then I worked the tip of the pliers under the remaining wire, my eyes turned upward toward the shadowy cornice and the gray of the open sky. I was determined to be on the safe side, no matter what circuits I had broken. All I thought of was to get the Shaler wire, and the bigger the mess I made of the others the sooner the Postal-Union would be sending their men to trace up the trouble. And with them would come discovery and safety.

It wasn't until I heard the girl's short, quick scream that I ducked and peered in, just as the steel jaws bit into the last wire and it was severed and swung dead from the cornice-edge.

VIII

As I looked, I saw the locked door burst open. Through it half-plunged, half-fell, the man in the quilted dressing-gown. He flung across the room, and I heard his booming cry of fury as he came. It was not an invalid's voice. Nor was his strength an invalid's strength, as he tossed the girl aside, like a rag, with one fierce jerk that sent her staggering against the pink- and green-papered walls.

The inside of the blackboard swung sharply up. I knew the sudden sickening sensation of sinking, helplessly sinking. Instinctively, I threw up my right hand, which held the pliers and caught at the edge of the eaves-troughing. The tool fell from my fingers. A moment later I could hear it clang and rattle on the iron and stone below. But I swung there, out over space, clinging desperately with both hands.

A rivet in the tin troughing slowly gave way: it drooped an inch or two lower with my weight. A second rivet broke, then it held true. I felt with my dangling feet for the blackboard. But the infuriated man had jerked it back into the room. He stood at the window, his face contorted with hate and rage. He balanced a revolver in his hand.

"You fool!" he gasped, as he thrust his arm out between the rusty iron bars. The corroded metal stained the sleeve of his

41

dressing-gown. For the first time a tingle of fear shocked every nerve in my body. I knew that he meant to shoot.

He laughed a little, devilishly, as he saw the terror on my face, motionless there, so close to his own. I shut out the scene, then an inspired thought came to me. With the quickness of the thought itself I kicked at his pointing revolver. That fierce kick, as it struck, flung the pistol from his hands, sent it rebounding against the wall, and carroming far out on the sod of the court below.

He looked at his bruised fingers a little stupidly. Then he looked at me, and laughed again, more wickedly than before.

"It's all the same, you fool," he gloated. And then I realised what he meant, for my arms were already throbbing, and I could feel a numbness creeping into my fingers. He meant me to hang there until the end. After all, it would be an end more horrible than the other.

The girl had failed me. She had fled or failed me, and was crouching there, too weak to act.

"Shoot! Shoot!" I gasped out to her. "Can't you shoot?"

"How can I?" mocked the devil at the open window. He knew, apparently, that nothing remained to menace him.

"*Shoot!*" I screamed, knowing the ordeal could not last much longer.

IX

The leering and relentless face still watched me from between the bars. Strangely enough, hanging there as I was, that face brought to my mind the thought of a hyena pressing against its cage. Then the thought vanished, for close behind the quietly exulting man, I saw the girl. Her face was white, like paper. Even her lips were colourless. Her staring eyes were expressionless with terror. For in her quaking and hesitating hand she held my revolver. I could see her slowly raise it to the level of the man's head. I could see the pale blue tint of the finger-nails compressed on the metal gunbutt. Suddenly, I felt like a spectator in a theatre-gallery, watching a drama far beneath him. I lost all sense of danger; I no longer remembered the ache in my arms, the scalding pain in my tortured finger-tips. I was conscious of only the scene before me—the scene that touched me with neither wonder, nor horror, nor regret. It seemed something taking place in another world. I simply watched and waited for the end.

The shaking revolver barrel was within a foot of the man's head before the picture shifted, quickly, like the shutter-plate of a kinetoscope.

"*Oh, I can't! I can't!*" screamed the girl, in abject terror.

The man swung sharply about at the unlooked-for sound of her voice. For the first time he saw and comprehended his peril. As he did so, he sprang toward her, and she in turn fell back.

I could hear the shuffling of feet on the bare floor, a muttered oath, the sound of quick, short gasps, and then the detonation of the firearm. A second later, a thin veil of smoke puffed from the open window. Then came the sound of something falling. Then the revolver itself dropped on the floor. I waited there for what seemed an eternity of time. Yet it must have been, in truth, little more than a second or two. I waited there, wondering which it had been.

It was the woman who tottered to the window. She leaned against the sill, panting, shaking. I could see her breast heave and fall, frantically. By this time my body was dead from the arm-sockets up. I could hold on no longer.

"The board! The board!" I gasped.

She must have understood, through her white-lipped terror, for she stooped dazedly and lifted the end of the blackboard to the window-sill, like a sleep-walker. Then she thrust it out, two feet, four feet, twice too far. I had no time to warn her, to have it withdrawn, though my weight, with such leverage, I felt, would surely overbalance hers. I had no chance even to see if her body rested on the inside end of the board. I could hold on no longer. My fingers relaxed, and I fell.

X

The outjutting blackboard sloped down and inward toward the window-sill. As I crumpled in across it, weak and exhausted, it caught and held me there, held me until my benumbed fingers recovered some ghost of their cunning and could clutch frantically at the board edged with oak. But as the board received my relaxing weight it quivered and dipped. Then it steadied, but still the outer

43

end slowly descended like the beam of a scale. It came to a level on the broad stone sill. There it balanced.

Below me I saw the iron-spiked fence and the stone of the courtyard. I panted and trembled, helpless, waiting and praying for strength. Then, inch by inch, I fought my perilous way in toward the sill—inch by inch, until I could clutch the nearest iron bar. As I did so, the outer end of the board went up again, and I slid forward down its smooth surface, down, down, slowly, deliciously, thankfully, until I touched the girl.

Then for the first time I saw that she had fallen across the board, motionless. She had fainted away.

I carried her to the window, and tore her waist open at the throat and fanned her frantically.

"Did I kill him?" she moaned, clinging to me, as she came to. For the first time I remembered, and looked around.

The wounded man sat on the bare floor against the wall, staring at us, stupidly. He held his right elbow in his left hand. But from where he supported it, the forearm fell straight down, limp, helpless. I could see the blood slowly dripping from his coat-sleeve, as I caught the girl and drew her away.

I'd already clutched the girl's arm in mine and snatched up the fallen revolver on the way to the door. How we got down those three long flights of stairs I scarcely knew. I carried the gun in my hand all the way. But no one opposed us, no one appeared. It seemed like a house of the dead. My hand still shook as I unlocked the great mahogany vestibule-door and swung it wide. And I could feel the girl clutch at me before the sudden apparition of the man in the green livery.

He stood with his back against the wall, his arms folded. His face was impassive but ominous, the eyes as cold and dead as Fate itself. But he made no move, for my gun was there confronting him. And I was more collected by this time, as I guardedly circled into the vestibule. But still the impassive mask showed no sign of the man behind it.

"Dickson," and I wheeled as I spoke so the girl stood behind me, "Your master's wounded, upstairs in the children's room!"

"Yes, sir!" answered the tranquil Dickson.

"Go there, quick. Then get a doctor. His arm is broken."

"Yes, sir," again answered the impassive lips. But I turned as he stepped forward, so that I might face him at each move. When he reached the stairs, I quickly swung the great, jail-like door shut and locked it. Beyond the outer door was the street, liberty, the open world.

"Are you ready?" I asked. "For you must go first and alone."

She looked at me curiously. The colour had come back to her face.

"I'm ready," she said, at last. Then she stopped and faced me in the gloom of the vestibule.

"I'll never forget," she said, with an odd little throaty shake in her voice.

"Not until to-morrow," I answered, a trifle bitterly, remembering what I had been through. Yet still again something in her eyes crept like wine along the veins of my tired body.

"*Never, as long as I live,*" she repeated solemnly. Her head drooped as she held out her hand to say good-bye. I took that hand in my own, knowing it was merely her sense of escape, her reaction after suffering, that made her speak. Yet I vaguely felt that life was confronting me with some moment to which I was unable to rise, that Destiny was in some way testing me, and finding me wanting.

"*I shall never see you again.*"

It was neither a question nor a statement, though it might have been either. Her face was quite colourless again.

"*Never,*" I answered, without hesitation. For the first time it came home to me how far her world had always stood from mine.

I think she felt what I said was true. She took one great breath, and looked up at me without a word.

"Good-bye," she whispered, as I unlocked the outer door, in silence, and held it open for her. She passed out and down the steps.

Two minutes later the great door closed again on me. It was raining softly and seemed late in the day. Down the quiet valley of brick and stone stretched the orderly rows of street-lamps. A stream of weary and sedentary labourers hurried east from Broadway, homeward after a day's work, little dreaming that behind the door, beside which I paused to make sure the coast was clear, I had been confronted by things not of their world. I plunged into their midst like a rabbit into a warren, suddenly remembering I was as hungry as a wolf.

CHAPTER THREE
THE ADVENTURE OF THE BLACK COMPANY

I

I waited on the corner of Broadway and Fortieth Street, lazily debating with myself whether it should be the Metropolitan or the Haymarket. I didn't care which, for those play-acting places seemed mostly a waste of time to me. When I wanted amusement, I always hankered after the real thing: I never cared to sit in a plush chair and watch a two-dollar picture of it. That make of mental cocktail was good enough for tired workers and hall-roomers. It was good enough for the souls of flat-dwellers who longed to obliterate their twelve hours of drab by a three-houred daub of melodrama. But when I wanted thrills, I preferred getting them from the jolts and bumps along the crazy, happy-go-lucky Under Groove itself.

So I stood at the curb, looking up and down the Rialto's crowded valley of lights, listening to its confusion of noises, lazily revelling in its panoramic tangle of life, detached enough from it all to enjoy it as a spectacle. For Broadway, from Forty-second Street south, was blocked—blocked just as I've seen a log-jam block a river. Motor-cabs and surface-cars, four-wheelers and hansoms for the theatres, broughams and landaus for the Metropolitan, glass-tonneaued autos and waggonettes from the uptown restaurants, all seemed hemmed and snarled together. Waiting crowds, on foot, blocked the street-crossings. Policemen waved and shouted and blew their whistles. Newsboys dodged in and out with the latest "extra." Chafing horses pounded the wet asphalt.

Then the key-log, whatever it was, at last gave way. The jam loosened; the two slowly disentangling lines of vehicles moved on again. Car-bells clanged, motors whirred and grunted and honked, dancing horse-hoofs tattooed and pattered on the muddy pavement. Then the line came to a second stop. Men in fur and evening dress looked out of the cab-doors impatiently. Women in white and cream and ermine leaned back on their cushions petulantly. A whistle blew; the line moved forward again, creepingly.

On a brougham door, drifting up nearer and nearer to where I stood, I noticed a white-gloved hand. As it came still closer, I saw that the sash had been lowered. Out of the hooded gloom suddenly appeared a woman's face.

I gazed at the passing face idly. It seemed strangely white in the black frame of the carriage door. It was a beautiful enough face, but I was most struck by its unhappiness. It was only one of many, I knew, oppressed with its joyless pursuit of joy.

The woman leaned farther forward, as her carriage wheels passed the crossing where I stood. She did not speak. But I could feel that she had swept me with one quick look. I saw the white-gloved hand move to the silver door-knob as our eyes met for the second time. A moment later, the door of the slowly moving carriage swung open. Not a word was spoken, but there could be no mistake about it. It was a sign, a signal. At some unequivocal yet inarticulate bidding I quickly stepped inside and closed the door.

II

The wheels did not rest; the creeping line did not stop. I sat back in the padded gloom—waiting, wondering. The only sound was a little gasp from the woman at my side. It was one of fear, or one of relief, I could not tell which. It might have been both. Then she half-rose from her seat and peered out through the curtained little back window of the carriage. There was something luxurious-sounding in the rustle of her wrappings, and a thin perfume of orris spread through the darkness about me.

"Were you seen?" she asked, and it wasn't until the sound of her voice reached my ear that I comprehended the actual tensity of her feelings, the nervous strain under which she was labouring.

"Seen by whom?" I asked, quite in the dark.

It was a moment or two before she answered my question.

"From the cab behind."

There was something so reassuringly low and full-toned in her voice that I felt half-ashamed of my lingering suspicions as she sat there beside me with her hands clasped in her lap.

"They're following me," she said at last, as though speaking to herself.

"Why should they?" I asked casually, still satisfied to wait for the cards as Destiny dealt them out. I had been taught to be wary, very wary, along the twists and turns of the Under Groove.

"You are a gentleman," she said, inappositely—I had always held that one of my particular calling could not dress too carefully—"You are a gentleman; I saw that the first time I passed you."

Then, indeed, she had passed me twice. The play was becoming more interesting. But I remained guarded and silent, wondering what freak of chance, or what coalition of forces, I was facing. I could not see her face distinctly in the dim light of the carriage. She apparently found it hard to continue, for she sat there at my side, for several seconds, perfectly silent.

"I ought to be in fustian, oughtn't I?" I ventured to bridge the awkward pause. "And, by the way, what *is* fustian?"

I knew she was peering at me in wonder. My note of levity seemed to puzzle her. I began to enjoy the suspense of it all. I even sat back, possessed by a wish to prolong the mysteriousness of the movement that had brought us together in that unlighted carriage. I even closed my eyes to consequences, for the moment, satisfied with the soft allurement of the situation. I began to dread her next speech, for I felt that with explanation would come disenchantment.

"I knew you would help me!" she said, and again she spoke the words half-meditatively, as though talking to herself.

More and more I began to dread, as I'd dread a blow, the earthlier touch that was coming closer and closer—the touch that was to prick and burst my bubble of momentary illusion.

I saw her suddenly stoop and grope in under the carriage cushions with her gloved hand. My own right hand went down and back as she did so. It is a trick that only the Under Groove ever teaches one.

"I want you to take this," she said. I saw she held a little packet in her outstretched hand. "It's nine thousand dollars in bank-notes, altogether. *I want you to take it and keep it for me.*"

III

I peered through the gloom at the woman. Then I peered down at the packet. I could just make out a tightly banded bundle of bank-notes, with their yellows and greens faintly visible through the drifting half-lights.

48

The woman was undoubtedly mad—as mad as a hatter, as mad as a March hare. My first fleeting impression was a desire to escape to the freedom of Broadway.

Suddenly an off-side automobile, backing round under the arm of an angry policeman, threw its searching acetylene glare straight into the hooded recess of the carriage.

It left her face cut out against the black cushion-cloth with the clearness of a cameo. It was a soft and slender oval of a face, crowned with a mass of hair too dark to be described as yellow, and yet too pale to be called golden. Her lips, at the moment, were tremulous and slightly parted. Her eyes were a clear brown, almost a seal brown, but now, apparently, big with some indefinable fear. Every line of her face was a line of breeding. Her teeth were very small, like rice, but also very white. Her face, as a whole, seemed to carry a spirit of audacity touched with weariness, of a youthfulness not without wisdom. Something about her gave me the impression of teeming vitality at ebb-tide, of a keen and tempered vigour of body sheathed in a momentary fatigue of spirit. She was still a young woman. She was also a singularly beautiful one. I decided to stay where I was. It is not every day that one can ride in a carriage with a beautiful woman as mad as a March hare.

She was still holding out the money for me to take. My hesitation, in fact, seemed to mystify her.

"But what am I to do with it?" I asked.

"Get away with it, at once, while you can," was her answer.

"Pardon me, but shouldn't you be a bit afraid of me? Haven't you your doubts about trusting me, I mean?"

"Even if I have it's too late now," she replied, after a little pause. I remembered what she had said about being followed. For the first time I realised that it might not be so easy as it had seemed to take and keep that little banded packet of notes.

"But what am I to do with it afterward?" I repeated.

She sat in deep thought for a minute or two.

"We could meet—yes, we could meet again, to-night," she murmured, holding a meditative finger against her lower lip.

"In what corner of the Fairies' Forest?"

She was thinking again, and did not answer me.

"No, I was wrong," she suddenly broke out. "*I* must get away from here. They will watch *me*, every move. They will follow me, every minute. That will leave you free."

"Thanks," I murmured. I was beginning to feel uneasy. I always like to know a little of the game before going into it.

"Listen!" she said, turning to me. I felt, from both her tone and her gesture, as her fingers touched my sleeve, that she was a young woman not above making the impersonal spirit of sex help toward the accomplishment of personal and selfish ends. "Listen. The driver outside has been ordered to go direct to 84 Wall Street. You can stay in the carriage and be taken there. They will never dream you have gone on. Then I can meet you there, sometime before midnight."

"But, madam—" I protested.

She had opened the chatelaine bag at her waist.

"Here are my keys. This one will open the office door."

"But what door? What office?"

"The office of the Black Company," she answered.

"But what right would I have in that office?"

"You would have every right," she said, thrusting the keys into my hand, "for the office of the Black Company is *my* office."

IV

There may have been nothing disturbing about the declaration in itself. What startled me was the memory that the figure at my side had seemed anything but that of a business woman, that she had impressed me as a contradiction of every idea of the commercial sphere of life. Here was still another incongruity; yet in some way it seemed to add to the ironic interest of the situation. That thin odour of orris greeted my nostrils again, as I turned to her.

"You haven't taken the packet," she said, reprovingly. Her lips were so close to my ear that I could feel the electric warmth of her breath. I had almost forgotten that we were being stalked, block by block, that we were being followed, every move we made.

"But what is this Black Company?" I asked.

The woman turned and peered out of the carriage window before she answered. I could see her face again, distinct in the drifting lights of Broadway. I tried to place that face, to fit it into its natural groove. But I could conjecture nothing adequate.

A new feeling of uneasiness, almost of terror, seemed to creep over her, as though she dreaded some final plunge, which could not further be put off.

"I shall tell you everything," she said, hurriedly, "if you will trust me and wait a little. There will be no danger on your part—not a shadow of harm will come to you. And you will be saving me misery and suffering, and perhaps worse!"

There was something strangely moving and appealing in her low-voiced, little cry for help, something blindly persuasive in her soft and feminine presence. I took her banded packet of paper with a reckless little laugh, and carefully buttoned the bills up in my inside breast-pocket.

"And wait for me," she said, as she peered out and drew her cloak about her. It was her glance and not her voice that told me I would be repaid for my trouble, as she turned back from the open door. Then, as the carriage passed Twenty-eighth Street, she murmured, "Good-bye," and dropped lightly from the step to the street, catching up and holding together in her gloved hand the voluminous folds of her skirt.

I saw her cross Broadway, hurrying eastward. Then the shadows of the side street swallowed her up. But from the little rear window of my carriage I beheld a black-hooded cab, not fifty feet behind me, swing sharply off to the left, in the direction the woman had taken.

The lights drifted by on either side of me. The streets of the lower town grew quieter and quieter. I could hear the ticking of the leather-cased coach-clock in front of me. I sat back in the padded seat, trying to think it all out.

V

Once inside the Black Company's office door, I felt more at ease and back in my everyday world. I had been sceptical as to the liveried coachman on the box, suspicious of the destination of the brougham, apprehensive of some hidden accomplice who might at any moment confront me.

51

But nothing untoward had happened. Even the patrolman on the corner of Broadway and Wall Street had given me nothing more than a casual glance. The very watchman had brushed by me without a sign.

Yet once inside that office and I knew my line of action was going to change. I intended to make my part no longer a waiting one. I first listened for a minute or two, to make sure I had not been followed. Then I satisfied myself the door was locked behind me. Then I struck a match and groped about for the electric-light switch.

I found it, beside a second door, on the opposite side of the room, and turned on the lights. The office about me was not unlike hundreds of other small offices in the crowded business districts of any city. On one side were several chairs, on the other a typewritist's table with a railing between, and above it an ordinary wall-telephone. The door leading to the inner office was locked, but one of the keys on my ring opened it. The second was a smaller room, but more luxuriously fitted up; a rug on the floor, a roll-top desk, three swivel-chairs, and, in the far corner, the looming black shadow of a safe. This, I saw, was to be a somewhat more interesting room.

As I have often said, sentiment and the particular calling I chose to follow never went well together. I had long since learned to eliminate certain hampering scruples, certain too costly feelings, from my make-up. I had a great deal to find out in that office, and not long in which to do it.

I began with the outer room. The only vulnerable object was the typewritist's table. The ring held no key for the drawer in that table. I had to pick the lock.

But I had only my pains for my trouble. The drawer contained a ream or two of unused paper, some rubber bands, a few dozen postage-stamps, a few hundred envelopes and a pair of black cotton sleeve-guards.

I closed the drawer, and then suddenly opened it again. For I had noticed, pencilled on its wooden edge, a series of figures. I took it, at first, for a telephone number jotted down for secret reference, but now partly scratched away. As I looked closer I knew no such numerals applied to telephoning. For I could make out: "37, back 28, on 113" . . .

I did not wait to replace the drawer, but dashed for the inner office, straight to the safe. It was a combination lock. The figures on the drawer-edge, I felt, were perhaps a fragment of the permutation which would throw its tumblers free and open the great black door. I schooled myself to calmness again, and returned to the outer room. There I copied down the figures, replaced the drawer, relocked it, and switched off the lights.

Back in the inner office, I drew the blind over the one small window, and locked myself in. Then I studied the safe, minutely, thoroughly, methodically, following my inspection with a page or two of figuring.

I found that, if the fragment of the combination I held was the correct one, so far as I knew locks and safes, there remained a little under three thousand throws, any one of which might be the right one.

I looked at my watch. I still had time, I felt, in which to do the work. Then I took off my coat and vest, for the office was close, rolled up my sleeves, and began.

VI

It took me exactly an hour and a quarter to get that combination. And it was an hour and a quarter of taxing and tedious work, with my ear against the lock-dials, trying to combine those permutations by the minutest distinction of sound, taking my cue from the slightest deviation from the normal ward-tap and tumbler-click, as I turned and tested and listened and turned still again. But I hit it in the end. The nickel knob at last relaxed under my feverish downward push of the hand, and the great door swung open.

I nursed no scruples and wasted no time. I had more reasons than one for finding out just who and what this Black Company might be.

That it was something slightly different from what its neighbours in that highly respectable business block took it to be was startlingly evident, as I made my examination of the safe. For, in the first place, beyond a few dollars' worth of postage-stamps, it held nothing of immediate market value. Other things it did contain, however, which in their own way, and for their own purposes, were not altogether worthless.

For in a leather-backed volume, very like an ordinary ledger in appearance, I found a long list of New York families of established wealth and position. So full was this list, that it might have stood for a Bradstreet or a "Who's Who" of the world of finance. The names were alphabetically arranged, the approximate amount of the fortune of each stated, the different properties, interests, and personal hobbies carefully entered. Following this was a column, in cipher, which was Greek to me, though preceding many of the names I noticed a blue cross, made in pencil, and before a few others a red cross.

In the next ledger I found a list of "subscribers," apparently those of the Black Company itself. In each case, the name and address were written in full, followed by certain cryptic figures. These subscribers seemed to be from every city and town of importance throughout the East, in both Canada and the United States.

In the next book which I drew out were pasted a number of newspaper clippings of advertisements. These fell like a ray of light on the perplexity through which I had been floundering. For the first advertisement read:

"Heiress, young, beautiful, to settle threatened estate legally must marry before September. Her trustees take this method to secure suitable husband, on whom they will settle $30,000 on day of marriage. Eligible gentleman, cultured, sincere, requested to write for particulars. No agents, no triflers or undesirables wanted."

Then came still another clipping, equally enlightening, equally persuasive. It ran to the effect:

"If the relatives and family of James E. (or James A.) Black, of THE BLACK COMPANY, Johannesburg, formerly of New York City, later of Damaraland and Johannesburg, South Africa, and recently deceased in Cape Town, will apply to Kolkner and Lincoln, duly appointed executors of THE BLACK COMPANY, 84 Wall Street, New York City, or to Messrs. Leavitt & Whitestone, 3094 Chancery Lane, London, W.C., they will learn something to their advantage."

Then followed a list of papers, obviously those in which the advertisement had appeared, with dates appended to each. Then came still another notice, inquiring, in the usual vaguely alluring formula, for the whereabouts of relatives and heirs of one John

Williams, who sailed for Australia twenty-two years before, and was there identified with certain mysterious mining ventures and smelting mergers.

Next came a huge package of cabinet photographs. It took only a glance to show they were portraits of the woman in the brougham. Then followed a Burke's Peerage, a Bradstreet, a well-thumbed *Almanach de Gotha*, and a package of business envelopes bearing the ensign: "Darius D. Cameron, Real Estate and Investments." Next, in a woman's handwriting, was a carefully compiled directory of European hotels, after many of which was a round "O" in black pencil; then a packet of letter-heads of "The Manhattan & Mattawa Development Company," carefully wrapped and tied with red tape.

I remembered that company; and it filled me with silent glee to behold its stationery thus coffined and sealed down. For, "The Manhattan & Mattawa Development" had died an untimely death, not a year ago. It had been nipped in the bud by the Post Office authorities at Washington, on the charge of using the mails for fraudulent purposes. And that business had been conducted by William Fernald, alias Charles Y. Leavitt, alias Henry Korn Kolkner. My ring of evidence was slowly but surely rounding itself out.

VII

Deeper in the safe I found a bundle of circulars. These circulars, I saw, as I opened them, had to do with the romantic and mythical heiress of the first advertisement, the heiress so distressingly in need of a husband. They had been sent out under the name of "The James Black Estate, Limited; Ezra Black, Albert Grosvenor Whitestone, trustees; Henry K. Kolkner, managing director, 120 Lombard Street, London, E.C." It was a very beautifully worded circular, setting forth that the aforesaid trustees were desirous of promptly and expeditiously obtaining a suitable husband for the heiress in question, artfully detailing the conditions under which the marriage of the said husband must take place. It would be one in name only, apparently, for the groom must meet his bride neither before nor after the ceremony. He was, indeed, at once to take up his residence in a certain State, and there remain until a divorce was secured. For this, the gentleman in question would receive a bank guarantee that the estate would pay over to him the sum of $5,000 on the day of the marriage, and the remaining $25,000 on the day the divorce decree was placed in their hands. The circular continued to state that necessary discretion had to be observed, to obviate undesirable publicity, and that an attorney-at-law would be furnished and all expenses met by the estate; and, also, as a guarantee of good faith, a strictly limited number of photographs of the aforementioned heiress had been made, and these would be forwarded to desirable applicants for the merely nominal sum of two dollars.

In other words, throughout the length and breadth of America, sober and workaday souls in shop and factory and office, idle and adventurous spirits, spirits of the lathe and plough and ledger, never dreaming they were nursing a suppressed and Vesuvian sense of romance, were to rein in their foolish dollars, by the hundreds, by the thousands. Then, the Black Company, having waxed fat on the fruits of its labour, would disappear from the face of the earth, only to reappear overnight in some new city and new guise.

I rummaged deeper into the safe, but nothing of value or significance met my eye. Then I turned to the cash drawer. There, instead of money, I found a .38-calibre revolver, fully loaded. Thinking things over, I decided to draw its teeth. So I shook out the cartridges, and from the end of each bit away the leaden ball. Then I relimbered the gun and restored it to its place. Then I stood there wrapped in thought.

Who and what was the queen of this Utopian love syndicate? Who actually was this woman, dangled so alluringly before the eyes of unsuspecting youth and romantic maturity and susceptible old age? That was what I now wanted to find out above all else.

I straightened up and looked about me thoughtfully. I saw to my surprise, that beads of perspiration were running down my face, that my hands were moist, that the room had grown hot and fetid. The rummage from the safe lay scattered in confusion about on the floor. I looked like a "yegger" interrupted in his work. I crawled into the open safe again, to make sure nothing had escaped me. But my search was unrewarded. All I found was a card with the address of a West Thirty-third Street tailor-shop pencilled on it, in a woman's handwriting. The face of the card was engraved in script, and merely said:

VIII

I sat down in the chair, contemplating that card, turning it over and over in my fingers.

"Mrs. Arthur Wheeler Swan." It was a goodly part of my duties to be versed in all records of importance that impinged on the Under Groove. And here I had, at last, stumbled on a name that meant something to me—it seemed to clang against memory like a rifle-shot against the bell behind a bull's-eye. It gave me a clue on which to work.

For Mrs. Arthur Swan was the English beauty who had been caught smuggling diamonds on the *Cedric*, with the stones carelessly tossed into the bottom of a smelling-salts bottle. Instead of sniffing at sal-ammoniac, she had periodically lifted seventy thousand dollars' worth of Amsterdam-cut stones, covered with ammonia, up to her disdainfully pretty nose. That, I remembered, was two years ago. Mrs. Arthur Swan, I also recalled, had been photographed and measured with that scrupulous nicety peculiar to the Bertillon system, and her record had been a subject of much newspaper talk at the time.

I sat looking at the card, contentedly, building up and piecing out that strange biography as well as it was known to the world. At last I had reached some key to the mystery into which I had drifted. This, then, was my sad and perfumed beauty of the closed carriage.

Then, of a sudden, I started up, galvanically, for the silence about me was torn by a terrifying peal of sound. It wasn't until I had leaped to my feet that I realised it was the telephone-bell ringing in the outer room behind me. I looked about in dismay. Then I glanced at my watch. It was already eleven. Then I ran to the outer room and guardedly took up the receiver and listened, without speaking.

"Hello! Are you there?" I heard a cautious and muffled voice asking.

It was the woman of the carriage.

"Hello," I answered, "Yes, I'm waiting here."

"What are you doing?" I thought I detected a note of suspicion in the query. It was caused, perhaps, by my delay.

I glanced across the room to the open door, apprehensively, as though the instrument before me had the additional gift of sight.

"I'm reading an evening paper for the third time," I answered, forcing a laugh.

"I'm sorry to be so long," answered the distant voice, in a more intimate whisper, "but I've been held here. They are just letting me go."

"I'll wait," I told her, as I heard her murmur of gratitude over the wire. Then a warning thought came to me.

"Will you be alone?" I queried, as casually as possible.

"Quite alone," she answered.

I hung up the receiver and went to work, carefully restoring everything to the safe. I closed the big steel door and relocked it, put the room to rights, switched off the lights, relocked the inner office door, sat down in the waiting room, and, with the evening paper in my hand, wondered what was before me.

It was well I prepared myself, for what I half-expected came true. As I sat there, the outer door opened without a sound, without the ring of a bell, the stir of a footfall, the click of a key.

The woman of the carriage, in her white Irish-point opera-cloak, stepped inside. She had done it very cleverly. It was the flowering of many years' practice at such things. In fact, waiting and prepared as I was, she startled me by her sudden and unheralded appearance.

Once inside, she turned and locked the door with her own key, without uttering a word.

IX

Then she faced me, brushing the hair back from her forehead and laughing a little. She now seemed more at ease, more triumphant. The unmuffled office light was a little harder on her. She looked older, less mysterious, more an alert and active woman of the world. But she still had the beguiling soft oval of face, the audacious red lips, the dreamy and shadowy eyes, the incongruous poise and bearing of a woman of breeding.

She sighed with relief as she saw me, feeling, I dare say, that her greatest danger had passed.

"Nothing has happened?" she hurriedly asked.

"Not a thing," I answered, with the politest suppression of a possible yawn. Then her quick glance swept the room. I thought I noticed a look of trouble leap involuntarily into her eyes. Then her glance coasted back to me, but she said nothing. I pretended not to see, and was holding my paper. She remained standing between me and the door.

"How can I ever thank you for all the trouble, for all the risk you have taken?" she said. There was a note of finality in her voice; it implied she was preparing for my dismissal. I bowed to it.

"Will you tell me just one thing, please?" I asked, taking out the package of treasury notes. She waited, with a nod of her head.

"I would merely like to satisfy a natural and legitimate curiosity as to where this money came from."

She looked at me very studiously, very guardedly.

"It isn't my money. It was merely entrusted to me for safe-keeping." This, I knew, was an evasion.

"But, madam, think of the circumstances! How am I to know this money was—er—come by honestly?"

She stared at me, the picture of offended dignity. But I knew the wheels of her brain were going like mad.

"It's too late to discuss that now, isn't it? The situation was rather complicated, wasn't it? You saw this; you came to my help; and now I am willing to pay you for it."

She was very clever. She was making me an accessory before the fact. She took out her key-ring as she spoke; a duplicate of the one I held, apparently. She unlocked the door of the inner office and switched on the lights. For the second time, I saw her face change, and I stood on my guard.

She wheeled, with her hand outstretched.

"Could I have the packet, please?" She spoke casually but I could distinctly feel that the situation had narrowed to the inevitable climax.

X

I said nothing, for the simple reason that I could think of nothing to say. But she drew her own conclusions. She was on her own ground now, and more sure of herself.

"Oh, if it's your pay you want," she said, with a shrug, turning to the safe and spinning the dials with the deft fingers of an expert, "I have enough here, I think," she added, still at work over the safe.

I watched her stooping back and its point-lace cloak in wonder. I could not quite see why she was bringing the safe into the situation.

When she stood upright again both her voice and her manner had altered. I caught the threat in her tones, the menace in her attitude.

"I am a woman alone in this office at midnight!" she cried.

"I'm quite aware of that," I retorted.

"I have reason to believe you are trying to rob me," she went on, pregnantly. "And more than that, I must ask you to give back every cent of mine you have taken, at once."

"And if not?" I ventured.

"If not, you fool," she burst out, with a grimace that contorted the beauty out of her face, "I'll kill you where you stand."

She wheeled, quick as a flash, and I saw the glimmer of the revolver from the cash drawer in her hand. She had me covered.

Her twitching face went white as paper when she heard me laugh, as I stood there facing her. For I knew I was blinking into a harmless barrel.

"Who are you?" she demanded, tight-lipped, taking a step forward.

"Who are *you*?" I echoed, without falling back an inch. Her attitude of mingled triumph and defiance suddenly angered me; I was getting tired of all this play-acting.

"I am a woman who will never let you rob her. I'm a woman who is going to protect what is honestly mine!"

I laughed in her face.

"I'll tell you who you are, now you have insisted on it. You are Blondie Bonnell, the craftiest confidence woman in America."

"You lie!" she cried.

"You are Mrs. Arthur Swan, whose photograph hangs in the Rogue's Gallery; you are the trumped-up heiress of the trumped-up Black Company; you are the accomplice of Albert Kolkner, who was arrested in London for conducting a criminal next-of-kin agency; you are the widow of John Williams, who was twice driven out of St. Louis for using the mails for fraudulent purposes; you are the fake Countess di Firasso, of the Denver Coleman case."

"You lie! You lie!" she gasped.

"You're more!" I went on, in a rage of indignation: "You're the hotel swindler the Pinkertons hounded out of Chicago for duping

60

Thomas, the cotton-broker, out of eight thousand dollars; you are the musical-comedy actress who began your career in London by stealing a pearl dog-collar from a Spanish dancer; you are the Carrie Kelly who evaded a Tiffany action for shop-lifting; you were put out of the Hotel Bristol, in Paris; you have been driven from Nice and Monte Carlo and Venice; an officer in Malta shot himself because of your trickery, your lies, the ruin you had led him to."

She gave a little gasp, and slowly lowered the arm with the revolver.

"You are the wickedest and the most unscrupulous woman in New York at this moment. You are the most dangerous criminal in America, because you are good to look at, and you trade on this; for under all your finery, you have nothing but the soul of a common thief."

"You lie!" she still cried, "You lie!"

"I do not lie and you know it, just as well as you know that you would shoot me like a street-dog, if you knew for certain that you had me cornered."

Her eyes narrowed and glowed at me out of her dead-white face, and her lips moved, but no sound came from them. She shook a little, with rage or fear, I could not tell which.

"Yes, I could," she whispered, thickly.

Like a flash, her right hand went up. It went first to the left side of my breast, just over the heart. Then, in what must have been an impulse or afterthought of fear, it moved on to my shoulder. The idea of cold murder was too much for her. All she wanted was to leave me maimed and helpless. Still again I had to laugh at the foolish irony of the whole situation.

Without warning, without hesitation, she fired her pistol point-blank at me. One, two, three, four, five times, she pulled the trigger. Each time the cap snapped and the grains of loose powder burned out in a feeble and impotent puff of smoke.

She stood looking at me, swaying back and forth. Then she sank back on a chair, covering her face with her hands. The pistol rattled down on the floor. I watched her. She was not sobbing; she was only waiting, planning, scheming, through all her artful pretence at tears.

She slowly lifted her head, at last, and looked at me searchingly.

"Oh, don't be hard on me!" she pleaded. I laughed a little. She gazed up at me out of wide and reproving eyes. I could see the shadow of some new resolve pass across her uplifted face.

"Do you know, I like you," she ventured, purringly.

Her efforts to be wheedling, her pallid blandishments, her tigerish writhes of conciliation, seemed almost piteous to me.

"Yes, I like you!"

"That comes too costly," I retorted. She winced.

"I mean it," she said, rising and coming nearer. I fell back from her. She turned away, and began pacing up and down the little room. Then she stopped.

"Give me a chance!" she pleaded. "I'll do anything—only give me a chance!"

She was back beside me again, coiling and wheedling. She was like a snake, at once loathsome and lovely.

"Is that what you told the man you got this money from?"

Her lips puckered and hardened in a sort of grimace of scorn.

"He was a fool—a vain and foppish old fool! He deserved to lose it! It's nothing to *him*!"

She stood still. "Why can't you be generous with me?" she still pleaded, regarding me with her half-averted face. Then, as she looked at me with her sidelong eyes her manner seemed suddenly to change. She swung squarely about and faced me; there was something peremptory in the movement.

"You won't listen to me?" she demanded, with some vague yet thinly veiled threat in her voice.

"I'm compelled to!" I retorted.

"But you won't do what I ask?" she went on, compressing her ever mobile lips.

"What can I do?" I equivocated, a little bewildered at her new line of procedure.

One minute later I knew what it meant. Before I could stop her she had started across the room—and even in her haste she lost no touch of her dignity—and came to a stop beside the office safe. She stood close to the wall, as she turned about, and I saw her finger play on an electric button there.

"Wait—stop!" I cried, springing foolishly toward her.

She only laughed.

"What's that for?" I demanded.

She laughed again, vindictively, desperately.

"That calls the watchman of this building—the night-watchman."

"Are you crazy?" I demanded, backing toward the outer hall-door.

But it was too late, and the woman knew it. She was cool and collected once more, and as I stood watching her it filtered through my brain just what her next move was to be.

"This will cost you dear!" I cried.

"I think not," she answered. "The watchman of this building knows me. He knows this office; and he will soon know that nine thousand dollars in treasury notes have just been taken out of that safe."

"Out of that safe?"

"Of course! From where else? And he will see that I am intercepting the thief who took them!"

"And what of that, Mrs. Arthur Swan?" I flung out at her. "What good will that do you, Mrs. Kolkner, *alias* the Countess di Firasso, *alias* Blondie Bonnell?"

She smiled a little wearily, a little listlessly.

"You forget that here I am Alicia Evelyn Black, that I'm a business woman in her attorney's office, a woman holding unimpeachable references! You forget that you secretly entered this office, *with keys that were not your own*, and opened that safe!"

I fell back a step or two, pondering what she had said. The woman was right. Who would believe the fairy story of this ridiculous adventure through which I had passed?

"You will, of course, be searched," she went on, more mockingly. "If the money is not found on your person, well and good, I suppose. If it *is* found there, you know the result. And we haven't more than one minute, I think, to get that stolen money back into the safe."

She shrugged her shoulders, carelessly, at my unconcealed resentment of her school-mistress-like tone. And still again out of this over-mottled life of mine I devoutly wished my record had been clean, simply to fight it out with her to the bitter end, for

63

the sheer sake of the fight. She had acted her part well, but her face, in the strong side-light, began to look tired and worn. Her eyes had lost their lustre, her colour had faded. She was a haggard and disillusioned woman, worldly-wise, cunning, crafty-minded, plotting and scheming for her tainted bundle of wealth, fighting for her miserable thief's swag.

I neither blamed nor hated her: I only pitied her. For I myself had often enough been swayed by the same capricious and incongruous passions. Some power not myself had dogged and driven me into paths that were darker even than hers—but through it all, the mystery of that tendency had remained impenetrable.

It was a sudden movement on the part of the woman before me that brought my thoughts quickly back to the present. Her gesture was one of impatience.

"Why are you taking such chances on this money?" I demanded, with my back against the door, waiting every minute for the steps on the stairs.

She studied me for a moment or two in perfect silence, without moving, before she answered.

"Do you want to know that?" she said, with still another complete change of manner, the incongruous look of tragedy falling unchecked and uncombated across her face.

"I do."

"Then listen," she responded, her artfulness once more forgotten. "The man I have worked and schemed and suffered for, the man I have endured all this for, is now a prisoner in the Tombs."

"For what?"

"He was arrested two days ago, and is being held there."

"But for what?"

"For passing what is claimed to be a forged check on the First National Bank!"

"And for how much?"

"It was for over eight thousand dollars," she dragged out, with what threatened to be a sob. I began to comprehend the situation.

"And if you make complete restitution this man will be set free, and perhaps no charges pressed?" I understood the bitter irony of it all, even before I heard her spoken words.

"Yes; then we can be together again."

"But why do you do this for a man of that type?"

Her answer, uttered a little scoffingly, a little resentfully, was primitive in its simplicity.

"Because he's the only thing in this life of mine that ever counted—he's the only thing I ever cared about!"

I could see the wave of passion, the sacrificial instinct of her sex, sweeping through even that sordid and tainted body.

"You poor, poor woman!" I said, as I looked at her white and weary face, with all its deepened lines of anxiety.

She caught her breath, as though she were about to break into tears. But her eyes remained dry.

I handed her the packet of notes. She let them lie in her lap unnoticed. Then I dropped the ring of keys beside them. For some reason or other I felt ashamed of myself.

"Put them in the safe," I gently commanded her.

She rose with a sigh and did so. There was neither triumph, nor exultation, nor joy, on her face.

"Now the watchman," I demanded. "What can we say to him?"

My one anxiety was to help her out.

She crossed the room, unlocked the outer door leading into the hall, and listened.

"You will not be molested by the watchman," she said simply enough.

"But you've called him," I reminded her. "We'll have to explain in some way!"

She locked the inner office door before she turned to answer.

"*He was not called!*" she said, as simply as before.

She eyed me steadily, in response to my stare of wonder. I was looking in the direction of the button she had pressed.

"That button is attached to the broken electric-buzzer there, just above your head." She pointed to the wall, then she crossed the room again.

There was something valedictory in her attitude as she opened the hall-door for me.

"And the check-forger, too?" I could not resist asking, with a meekly comprehending nod of the head toward the broken buzzer.

She did not answer in words; but I found myself growing hot and cold up and down the backbone, under her sudden little scoffing laugh.

"You clever, clever woman!" I said humbly, with my hat in my hand.

CHAPTER FOUR
THE ADVENTURE OF THE PRIVATE WIRE

I

I leaned back in the big rotunda chair, a week later, and yawned. Then I took out a cigar, and yawned again. I began to wonder if, after all, there was so much fun being in a big city unless you're mixed up with big affairs. I next pondered the question as to whether or not even contact with big affairs was enough, when the affairs happened to prove bigger than your own resources. Then I meditatively and ruefully struck a match.

Now, provided a man's not following the Guy Fawkes line of business, striking a match in the well-padded armchair of a well-guarded Broadway hotel is not exactly a Great Divide in the dull hours of a long morning. "But w'en you're spreadin' nitro-soup," as Dinney once put it, "you don't want to bite your caps too close!"

For before this particular match had burned half-way down, a large-bodied, quietly dressed stranger in the chair at my elbow said: "Could I trouble you?" I said, "Certainly," lazily, without so much as looking past the tip of his extended cigar. But I saw it was a coffee-coloured perfecto with a life-band. It had a soothing kind of smell about it, I noticed, as the light caught, the match burned out and I flung the stub away.

"Thank you," said the stranger, as he leaned back in his chair with a contented sigh. I smoked on in silence. From the little wire cage beyond the news-stand I could catch the click of the telegraph key. I almost envied that red-headed operator in that little hyena-den of a work-room. Life was still worth while for him; it gave him something to do.

I'd been so lonely in that big onyx-pillared place of painted stucco and crimson and gilt that I'd even struck up an acquaintance with that red-headed rotunda operator. When he found I'd once worked the wires myself, he opened up and told me how his arm had given out after five years with the Postal-Union, how he'd shifted to news-bureau receiving, and how he'd dropped to this lady-work on a hotel wire. And I knew, as I listened to his send, that he was a "has-been."

"This is the limit!" ejaculated the stranger at my elbow.

I looked 'round at him for the first time. It was not a melting look, for I always had my suspicion of possible pick-ups. But he only laughed back at me, over the time-table he held in his hand.

He was a man of about thirty-five. He looked like a well-to-do business man, well-poised, well-groomed, with the affable carelessness of a man who knows he's alive and prosperous. His face was lean and deeply lined, but well-formed. The line of his mouth was a little cynical, perhaps, but New York had made me used to that look of his. His eyes were small and gray, but quick-moving. They seemed to give his face a bland and humorous turn that set me more at ease. His ears, I noticed, were large and red, with their lobes pinned close to his jawbone. His face, on the whole, was the prosperous, jocosely mournful and youthfully old American business man's face.

"This *is* the limit!" he proclaimed aloud, as he saw me still staring at him. And still I stared, without a word, though he saw, or pretended to see, some shadow of a question on my face, for he swung around in his big chair and faced me.

"Do *you* know anything about these Chinese puzzles?" he asked, putting the time-table before my eyes.

"Not much," I admitted.

"I want to get up to Middleburg, New York," he went on, with unruffled friendliness. "It's somewhere in Schoharie County. But I'll be hanged if I can find what road I take west from Albany, or where I strike the Delaware and Canal Company's line, and where I leave 'em for the Cooperstown and Charlotte Valley branch."

I began to laugh. His dilemma was such an out-and-out one. He looked at me questioningly.

"I used to know something about things like that," I confessed.

"Well, I don't!" And he, too, grinned a little.

"Will you let me look over that time-card of yours?"

He gave it to me, and I bent over it, but I still kept one eye of attention on the stranger, though I felt a little ashamed of my suspicions.

"It's like a game of Pigs-in-Clover!" he sighed, leaning back and puffing at his cigar. The house detective drifted by, and was lost in the crowd.

"You take the D. and C.C.'s line west from Albany," I explained to the man beside me. "Then you'll have to change at Central Bridge for the C. & C.V. and then go south to the town you want!"

"Could I make it to-day?"

I bent over the time-table still again.

"You'd better take the midnight, and catch the morning train out of Albany."

"That means another whole day in this town!" and he smothered his disgust in a yawn.

I folded the time-table and handed it back to him.

"You're a railroad man, aren't you?" he suddenly inquired, more intimately.

"I used to be on the old Flint and Père Marquette, up in Saginaw," I admitted.

"Saginaw!" he exclaimed. "Then you must know Pugh and Crombie and Simpson?"

The names were not familiar to me. I guardedly explained that it had been several years since I left Saginaw. I say I did this guardedly, because I had never yet found out the reason for my own leaving; and I was still afraid of him.

I think he smelled a rat, for there is nothing so suspicious as suspicion.

We smoked on in silence for a minute or two.

"You're tied up for to-day?" he essayed carelessly.

I confessed that I was. He seemed relieved to hear it. Then he yawned and stretched his legs.

"Let's get out o' here and kill some time!" he suggested, off-handedly, without so much as a glance to see how I'd take it.

I was about to answer, when I heard my name called out through the big rotunda. I was being "paged" by the hotel office. I could see the blue-coated, yellow-braided bell-boy, with his little square of nickel, and I could see the tinted telegram-envelope he held between his thumb and the tray-bottom. I could hear him calling out my name, over and over again, as he went in and out among the crowd. When he came within hailing distance, I stopped him. I felt like something and somebody in the world, after all.

I could half see the man at my elbow eyeing me as I tore open the envelope. But I handled that despatch with care, for I felt sure it must be a message from Dinney. The stranger still watched me, through his cigar smoke, as I unfolded the sheet of yellow paper.

Then I read the message through, carefully, slowly, contentedly puffing at my cigar as I did so. What I read was this:

> *The man you are talking to is Paddy Miron, the smoothest come-on man in New York.*
> THE KEY OPERATOR.

II

I must have laughed a little without meaning to do it, for he turned on me sharply with a new look in his eyes that made them almost ratlike. It was my turn now to smooth things out.

"There's luck for me, all right!" I cried, waving the message in front of him. I could see his hungry eye follow each move of the paper. But he got no chance to read it.

"That partner of mine has clinched it! He's put through our mining deal—Temagami and Nipissing silver claims to the Guggenheimer interests!" I explained, as I folded and pocketed the despatch. I knew my bait had brought him up, for the quick flash of his eyes was like the belly-flash of a startled fish.

"Are *you* in on those Cobalt claims, too?" he inquired, settling back again.

I chortled and patted my pocket-wad. "There's just six thousand for a six weeks' rake-off!" I gloated.

"Good!" he said, languidly. Paddy Miron, I saw, was not the worst actor on Broadway. He was studying his train-card indifferently by this time. Then he linked his fingers at the back of his head, once more stretched his legs, and looked the picture of ennui. I waited for the next move, sizing him up. Physically, I had nothing to feel particularly confident about. I was outclassed, obviously, as to weight. But I still felt that I might be able to hold my own, if things came to such a turn.

He looked at his watch lazily, then he looked at me with the light of a new inspiration on his face.

"If we've both got to kill time here," he suggested, "let's go down to Resicza's for some o' that Hungarian *goulash* of his."

"That sounds good!" I admitted.

I pushed the bell set in the onyx pillar behind me, calling for telegraph blanks. I made it a point to write my message small, when the boy had brought the blank, for I knew the eyes of my new-found friend were following every move of my pencil.

"Thanks for the tip," ran my despatch. "Tell the house detective to keep off, for I want to follow up the game."

I watched the boy make his way back to the hotel office, and then on to the hyena-cage, where the sounder tapped and clattered. The other man beside me did the same. I could see the disquiet that crept into his face, so I chuckled a little, to ease him down.

"We're going to double our money in that silver stock—we're going to *triple* it, if this goes through! And then I guess we'll show this old town a thing or two about spending."

"Wonderful how the wire helps business out," essayed my friend, meditatively.

"It is," I assented, for I had just heard the hyena-cage operator rap out a brisk Morse "O.K." to me across the crowded rotunda. What was more, he had succeeded in throwing a touch of humour, of quietly hilarious comprehension, into his metallic dots and dashes. The man at my side was venturing some still further ruminative and impersonal remarks about the mystery of the wire.

"Hanged if I could ever understand how telegraphing is done," I observed, quite as meditatively. And I saw his face brighten at that casual admission. It was only a minute and guarded change, but it was there. And it continued to rest there, I thought, as we made our way out of the crowded hotel rotunda, and stepped into a cab and went rattling down Broadway, swinging sharply 'round into one of the lower side streets toward Sixth Avenue. Then we alighted and went down a narrow little stairway into a gas-lit hall, and from there into a subterranean eating-room with a row of tables down one side. The place was almost empty, so we had our choice of tables.

It had its fascination, this stalking the stalker, but for the first time, in the light of that vile-smelling Hungarian cellar, I wondered if I hadn't gone a little too far in the business, for as I ordered cigars and Karlowitzer I caught the flash of some mysterious message between Miron and the yellow-haired ogre behind the bar. It was only a glance, but in that glance I knew a message had been given and received.

We sat there smoking, apparently as happy as two ducks in a ditch; but we weren't. I was watching Miron, and Miron, I knew, was watching me. The man behind the bar it was impossible to keep under my eye as he came and went. He could have worked a dozen ropes without my seeing him do it, but I sat there, satisfied, waiting for the next move.

"Why the devil d'you carry so much loose money around with you?" my new-found friend reprovingly demanded. He had just watched me flash my roll, for I had insisted on paying as we went. I felt that it was worth it.

"It's only a few thousand."

"But it's not safe in a town like this!"

"Oh, pshaw; I like to have it handy."

He looked at me studiously. I suppose a fine, big Cheshire cat contemplates a cornered mouse with a good deal the same sort of look. And while he still bent that look on me, I was dimly conscious of a third man entering the place, although my eyes were fixed on the ash at the end of my cigar. I glanced up, at last, and he came straight for us. After all, I saw there wasn't going to be much of a stage-wait.

The newcomer hurried straight up to Miron. He jerked a chair from the next table and flung himself into it.

"Thank Heaven!" he cried, pushing back his hat. "I've been scouring the Island for you!"

He was a young man, yet not an innocent-looking young man. He was as tall and muscular as a sparring instructor, though there was more humour than brutality in his cautiously easy-going face. His clothes were cut like a college-boy's—turned-up trousers, tan shoes, a striped band of corded silk on his soft hat, and a coloured shirt.

"This is Mr. Gahan," Miron was saying soberly. "Mr. Gahan, my friend Mr. Mahler—Mr. Richard Mahler."

Young Mahler acknowledged the introduction with a curt and diffident nod. Not once did he condescend to turn his eyes in my direction.

"I want to see you alone," he said to Miron. He was still more or less excited.

Miron shrugged his shoulders. I suppose he meant by the movement that good form demanded I should not be either left alone or shut out from their confidence.

"But I tell you this is important!" cried the younger man.

"That's all right!" answered Miron, soothingly. "Mr. Gahan's a friend of mine—he stands in on anything that's open to me!"

"But this is a personal thing, I tell you!" insisted the newcomer. He caught up his watch and looked at it, with a great show of hurry.

"Then let's have it," demanded Miron. "Two is only one extra."

We drew in closer round the little *café* table. A sense of mystery crept through the smoke-tinted air. For the first time in a whole week I felt that I was alive. But I warned myself to keep awake and watch.

"*We've tapped the Winnett wire!*" said Mahler, almost in a whisper. I saw the other man's hands begin to shake with excitement. A little tingle of nerves played up and down my backbone. Perhaps, after all, it was true; but I sat back, watching the drama. For, history or farce, it was good drama.

"We cut in on his wire two hours ago," rattled on Mahler, and as he continued to speak, he tapped on the table with his long, lean forefinger for emphasis. "We've got him where he can't get away. Every Gravesend and Jamaica race-report that goes up to that pool-room is going in on our key. It comes to us first, we hold it up, and then we cut in and send it through again when we're good and ready."

"Great Heavens!" cried Miron; "that means you can soak 'em for ten thousand—for twenty thousand, if you like!"

"It means more. It means we can get our tips, spread our money and place it and then pull in on the long shots, *to the limit*. It means that we can rake in, not twenty thousand, *but forty thousand apiece*!"

IV

"Phew!" gasped Miron. Then he felt an apparent enough qualm of doubt.

"But how do I know this is all on the square?" he demanded.

"Come and see it with your own eyes. Come and see it. Come and hear it, and if you don't like it, keep out."

Miron still pondered. "When do those returns start coming?"

"They've started now. We're losing time, good time."

"But even though you *have* cut in on the Winnett wire, as you say, how am I going to get my money up, once I get a sure tip?"

"It's like rolling off a log. And I've *told* you that already. I get the race returns and hold 'em up. You're in Grinnell's with the money ready, holding down the booth and waiting for my 'phone call. As soon as I get the despatch in on my relay, stealing it off the wire that goes up to their pool-room, I ring you up by 'phone. Then I give you the returns of the race that has already been run, holding it back from Winnett's. You walk into his pool-room, make your bet, get your slip, and sit down and wait. Then I send through the delayed returns, and they're chalked up. You go to the paying-teller's two-by-four wicket, get your money and walk out again. Isn't that clear enough?"

Miron began to see things more plainly, and to show more interest.

"And how much could I make? In one go, I mean?"

"That depends on how much money you've got in your mitt at this very minute."

Miron took out his roll and looked it over. "I've only got two thousand dollars," he announced, dejectedly.

"Well, you know what two thousand on a ten or twelve to one shot amounts to, don't you?"

Miron pounded on the table with his fist.

"I'm in on this!" he cried with sudden conviction. "I'm in on this, to the limit."

"Of course, I've got to have my percentage!" interposed Mahler.

The older man drew back again. "How much?"

"Two per cent, on the whole field."

"That's easy!" Miron, relieved, turned to me. "What d'you think of this, anyway?"

"It sounds great," I admitted.

"But I'm from Missouri—I've got to see the goods," said Miron, weakening again.

"It seems straight enough," I argued. I was, apparently, ashamed of his timidity.

"One minute—is my friend in on this?" demanded Miron, with a hand-wave toward me. Artfully, circuitously, the web was spreading.

"How much has he got?" asked the other diffidently.

"I've got a good six thousand, and got it here!" I retorted.

"I s'pose he is, then," Mahler assented. Yet his tone wasn't genial.

"But no one gets percentage out of me until I see this wire-tapping machinery at work," I declared, taking my stand.

"Keep out of it, then!" Mahler's lip curled. Was he trying to let me out? Or was he luring and leading me on, with this side-stepping coyness of his?

"He's right enough," Miron argued with the wire-tapper. "I know you're on the square, Mahler, but business is business. You get no rake-off until we see the goods."

"Great Heavens!" scoffed Mahler, "then come and see them! Don't sit here cackling like an old hen all day! *Do* something, for we've got a gold mine leaking away!"

Miron threw me a knowing look. It seemed to say, "Shall we try it?"

I nodded. Two minutes later, we were up out of the *café*, in the street once more.

V

We climbed into a waiting hansom, the three of us, and dashed for Broadway.

I sat in the centre, on the edge of the seat, Miron and Mahler on each side of me. This left me squeezed in between their knees, considerably in front of them. I didn't like the position, but I kept my eyes open, and also my ears. I began to feel the need of this, when it suddenly came home to me that Miron was cautiously fingering the outline of something in my hip-pocket.

A Chicago tailor had made that pocket, hiding it in the hollow of the back and padding it out cunningly. But a revolver is a hard thing to hide, even when the barrel is sawed off short, after the style of the Yegger. I could feel the look that flashed back and forth between the two men. There wasn't a sound, there wasn't a move. But one man had telegraphed a warning and a question to the other. There was no use trying to evade the situation, so I pushed in closer between them on the edge of the cushioned seat.

"My gun jab you at all?" I asked, airily enough.

"Your *what*?" cried Miron. He was a good actor.

"My revolver," I answered, putting my hand back on the padded pocket.

"Why—what the devil are you toting a thing like that around *this* town for?" he demanded.

I'd spotted his own artillery an hour ago. I felt like putting the same question to him, but second thought told me to keep quiet.

"That's mining-camp life for you!" I laughed back. "You get the habit out in those Western holes, and you keep your hip sore rubbing against car-seats when you come East."

Mahler looked relieved, though it seemed to me the older man still worried about that gun. As we swung off Broadway into one of the lower West Twenties, Mahler spoke.

"Shaler's in on this, you know!" he hurriedly explained.

"Shaler!—how'd you get *him*?"

"Over the 'phone at the Athletic Club. He's good and sore on Winnett."

The name of Shaler took me back, at a bound, to the girl of the Unknown Door. It may have meant nothing, but it was at least a new element in the play.

I had no time to think it over, however, for we had drawn up in front of a shabby, four-storied, red-brick building. It was dark-shuttered and unkempt and forbidding of front, and I noticed a tarnished brass dentist's sign on the door.

I followed the other two men up the steps and in through a dark and tawdrily carpeted hall. From the back of this hall we entered a large, shabby genteel, old-fashioned room that smelled of creosote. At one end I saw a dentist's chair, and beside it a stand of instruments. Behind this instrument-stand stooped what might be the dentist himself, a fat, white-skinned man of about forty. He was bald and he carried a very shifty and unstable eye in his head. Once he made out who we were, he stood upright, and gave his attention to cleaning a set of drills.

"Where's Shaler?" asked Mahler, circling the room with his quick glance.

"Hasn't turned up yet!" mumbled the man at the drills.

Mahler's face fell. He looked toward the back of the room, walled off by a Japanese folding-screen over-scrolled with rushes and flying storks in gold.

"Then we can't wait for him!"

"Who's Shaler?" I made bold enough to query.

"He's young Shaler, railroad-king Shaler's son, the nerviest young plunger in New York—and he especially wanted to get in on this."

I, too, I promptly decided, especially wanted to get in on this. And I formed a picture of the youthful plunger in my mind's eye. I once more peered about the room, and decided that young Shaler was luckier than he imagined.

"Let him stay out!" growled Miron. "We don't want all Broadway in on this!"

And I should have felt flattered, for Miron's declaration plainly implied that I was meat enough for anybody.

VI

Mahler swung the screen to one side. Behind it stood a big deal table covered with green baize. Scattered about on this table were a couple of switches, a costly pony-galvanometer, such as might be used in a big office to measure wire trouble, a condenser, a one-half duplex set, dry batteries, a key and sounder, and a few yards of number twelve wire. The relay was attached to two wires covered with green insulating tape. These wires dropped from the table-edge, trailed across the back of the room, and disappeared through the window-sash at the rear of the building. I had my own suspicions as to just where they ran after that; and by hook or crook, it was my duty to verify these suspicions.

"Has anything gone through yet?" asked Mahler, swinging round the table.

"The scratches and jockeys and weights went through for the Jamaica events," answered the man, cleaning the nerve-drills. "They're on the card there!" Then he went on with his work.

Both Miron and Mahler bent over the card, studying it. I indulged in a careful scrutiny of the room as they did so. Then both men looked up together, for the door-bell had rung. A sense of suspense filled the place.

A moment later, a very warm and excited-looking young man had stepped inside. He seemed little more than a youth of twenty-one, open-faced, clear-eyed, well-nurtured, and strangely out of place in that thick and grimy atmosphere. He wore a scarab pin and gold cuff-links, and his fingers were a little stained from cigarette-smoking. He mopped his forehead as he came in; he was plainly labouring under great excitement. It wasn't until the light from the back-windows struck him full in the face that he seemed less ingenuous, less unsophisticated, than I had first judged. But I surmised it was Shaler, even before he spoke.

"Can we get 'em?" he cried, ignoring my presence.

"Get 'em?" answered Mahler, with a laugh, where he bent over the relay. "Just listen to this!"

His long, lean fingers toyed for a second with the armature lever, and then he shut the switch. The little piece of brass screwed to the table seemed stung into sudden life, and as it clattered and pounded out its dots and dashes I saw Shaler watching it, fascinated.

I didn't dare look at Miron. I didn't feel sure enough of myself to glance at Mahler. For, instead of listening to the crisp, businesslike "send" of a race-track expert I was listening to something that sounded like the broken and doddering mumblings of imbecility. It wasn't even good Morse. It could only be the jolts and spasms of a ham-operator, who had taken his third lesson in a correspondence school of telegraphy. It was a cheap "super" in the room above, working the far end of what was obviously a mock circuit.

"These are the rest of the weights and entries," explained Mahler to the boy and me. "The races start going through any time, now."

"I had a deuce of a time getting this eight thousand," complained young Shaler, as he dragged his gold-initialled wallet from an inside pocket. "I couldn't let the governor on, and, of course, old Silverthorn wouldn't advance me another *sou*."

The two men eyed the money hungrily. I almost began to feel sorry for the boy.

"Of course, I wouldn't do this," he protested, counting off his notes, "if Winnett hadn't gouged that three thousand out of me! He didn't play a straight game that time, and I'm going to get even with him. I tell you, it's coming to me!"

"Of course it's coming to you!" purred Miron.

I couldn't help thinking how much that speech of affronted innocence lashing itself into a fury reminded me of Dinney and his sophistries. "Why shouldn't I be on the make this way?" Dinney used to ask. "I tried to do it honest, and they never gave me a decent chance! And I guess this world owes ev'ry man a livin'! If I could get it straight, I'd take it straight, but if they won't give it that way, I'm goin' to take it the other way!"

It was the same old and shallow self-deceit, the same old salve for the sore conscience, the weakling will; the same old whine of the man who'd never learned to make offence against law a philosophy of conduct. As for myself, I used to read Nietzche in my younger days: but now I *acted* him. I saw clearly enough to what end that path led. I never screened myself in sentimentalities. I had no illusions as to my final escape. If I could not be honest with others, I could still be honest with myself. Some day, when the end came, I'd have to pay, and pay well. But until that end I accepted my individualism—if you care to call it that—for exactly what it was worth, claiming my right to live by the sword, until by that self-same sword I should some day die.

VII

So I studiously counted over my money before my two fellow-adventurers. I was probably small fry to them by this time, and might also be hard to handle, but I should at least make it interesting before they could land their bigger catch.

"I'm still in on this, of course?" I demanded, with a show of anxiety, yet cudgelling my brain for some clearer line of action. I could see the two men exchange glances, with still another question and answer as quick as wireless.

"Of course you're in," said Mahler. "We can simply bunch the pile so Winnett's men won't get suspicious."

"I don't give a hang about the money, you know," broke in Shaler. "But I *do* want to get even with that crooked layout!"

"Well, it's money *I* want!" I declared to the circle about me. The young man looked at me and laughed disagreeably when I had delivered myself of this declaration. For the second time I noticed that he wasn't quite so young as he had seemed.

"We're wasting time, gentlemen!" cried Mahler.

I sauntered back to the window on the left of the table.

"Who puts the money up over at the pool-room?" I asked, sitting on the sill.

"The wire's all I can handle!" protested Mahler, petulantly.

"I don't want to mess up with other people's money!" likewise protested Miron. Shaler looked blank at this show of reluctance.

"You've got to!" he cried, "or this whole thing falls through."

"But who decides which horse to bet on?" I demanded.

"The wire decides that," retorted Mahler. "We take the entry giving us the longest shot."

"Listen!" said Miron, hurrying over to the relay. Mahler was after him, in a moment, and as the current opened and broke, the little metal lever under his eye fluttered and jigged and danced, filling the quiet room with sound.

"You've got to get that money up, and get it up quick!" the alert-eyed Mahler warned us.

"Well, I'll do it, if I've got to," said the equally artful Miron, with a second show of reluctance.

VIII

Miron stood across the table from me, on the right. Shaler was directly in front of the table, facing Mahler, stooping over it from the back. I started toward Miron, with the roll of bills in my outstretched hand, before Shaler could reach him. Mahler still bent over the key. As I stepped across the room at the back of the table, I planted the sole of my foot squarely on the two little green wires that ran across the carpet from the operating table to the window-sash. As I stepped forward, I kicked sharply with my right foot, in a feint at stumbling, and then scrambled up, grinning sheepishly.

A cry broke from Mahler, an impatient oath from the older man. For the sounder stopped, dead. At one stroke I had torn away their wires. The super in the room above was pounding a useless and inarticulate key.

I didn't exactly like the look that sprang into Miron's face. But I was ready and waiting, if the worst came to the worst.

"You cow! You've killed the whole game!"

"Can't you fix 'em?" I asked, eyeing the trailing wires.

"Fix 'em?" mocked Miron, ash-coloured with anger.

"Yes; can't you tie 'em together again?"

My placidity left him speechless, guttering like a turkey-cock. Mahler was the first to recover himself. He meant to fight it out.

"It'll take fifteen minutes to get that connection," he cried, springing toward the door and calling for the man at the dentist's chair to follow him. Then he turned to Miron. "You push those wires up through the window again—I'll get to the roof and cut in on the same line. Then we can catch the fourth race, anyhow!"

Miron caught up the loose wire as the door closed, and thrust it out through the window, Shaler closely watching him. As he did so, I quietly reached out my hand, caught the armature-lever screw of the relay between my thumb and forefinger, and quickly twisted it tight until it bit into the metal. Held thus rigid, no current could startle it into movement.

"Now, boys, if I'm to manage this for you—" said Miron, briskly, swinging round to the table.

"But they haven't cut in!" I complained, to gain time.

"The deposits, please!" said Miron, with a touch of impatience.

"But that little clicker thing isn't going!" I insisted.

"It'll go when it's needed," said Miron, swinging back to the window. Then he thrust out his head and called to some one above: "Have you got it?"

"Yes; doesn't she break?" came Mahler's voice, muffled and far away.

"Not yet!" answered Miron. And I could hear Mahler's curse of perplexity. Then, in afterthought, he called down again: "Get your money ready for your bets—I'll have it through by that time."

"Now, gentlemen," said Miron, suavely. But I could feel the claws under the velvet of his voice as he caught up his hat and faced us.

I turned to Shaler, whose thoughts seemed to come by freight. "I don't see why we should put up good money until we see something doing!" I protested, throwing him a look that passed completely through him.

"Why, aren't you going to bet?" he cried, his face falling.

"No, I don't think I am," was my placid reply, and to show how much at ease I felt about it all, I took out a cigar and lighted it. But by the time it was lighted, Miron stood between me and the door.

"You came into this game, and you've got to put it through, and put it through quick!" he ripped out.

I knew by the look on his face that all pretence and acting were over. It was man to man now, to the finish.

"That's what I intend to do," I answered.

"Then what're you quibbling and welching about? What reason have you got for blocking this game, and keeping this young man out of his money?"

I looked at him through the drifting and curling cigar smoke. He made a fine apostle of the oppressed, a fine defender of the weak. And I was just in time to see him craftily transfer a handkerchief-covered piece of metal from his hip-pocket to the right-hand pocket of his coat.

"It's not much of a reason, but it's enough for me."

"Well, what?" he was getting uglier every minute.

"It's merely that telegram I got in the hotel-lobby this morning!" I unfolded the yellow sheet in front of him, and contemplated it blandly.

"What *is* your telegram?" he demanded, still keeping the tail of one eye on the fidgeting and mystified Shaler.

I handed the slip of yellow paper to Miron. He took it without so much as lowering his eyes to it. He was on his guard now, too much on his guard to lose his drop on me. But I suppose it was my unruffled and placid self-assurance for that silent minute of tableau that exasperated and unnerved him, for with a little guttural grunt, almost of defeat, he turned to the sheet of yellow paper and slowly read it.

IX

He read it in silence. Then, apparently, he read it again, and still again. I could see his lips move; but for several seconds he did not look up.

When he did look up, my own right hand was in my coat-pocket, and my forty-four, blue-barrelled, sawed-off Colt was there, pointing directly at his breast.

"Well, I'll be—!" he breathed out, slowly. It was neither fear nor rage nor disappointment. It was only utter disgust.

He still stood there, chewing his lower lip, meditatively. I buttoned up my coat. Shaler looked from one to the other, mystified.

"When are we going to get those bets up, anyway?" he complained, "and what are you fools still rowing about?"

Still again Miron and I looked at each other, face to face, for several seconds. Then he peered at my right pocket, then once more back at me. It wasn't merely a look; it was a duel of wills, a contest of audacities, a silent and motionless battle.

"All bets will have to be off for to-day!" he announced, brusquely, holding the door for us.

Yet it wasn't until we were in the open street that Shaler looked at me with any show of personal interest.

"Will you kindly tell me just why you didn't bet that roll of yours?" he demanded, as we started toward Broadway.

He seemed already more of a man, away from that tainted atmosphere.

"Those wires were dummy, you fool!" I cried out. "It's all a fake, a come-on, a con game, a bunco, through and through."

"I knew all that," said Shaler, lighting a cigarette.

"You knew it?"

"Certainly."

"Then what—what were you after in there?"

"Evidence," said Shaler, glancing down at his watch. Then he swung about and hailed a passing hansom.

"Evidence?" I echoed.

"Yes, evidence," he repeated with a touch of disgust. He turned half-way 'round on the hansom steps. "I'm Hallen, the pool-room man your Commissioner brought over from Boston to stir up Doogan's office—*and you've dished my first week's work.*"

CHAPTER FIVE
THE ADVENTURE OF THE TIME-LOCK

I

At any other time the thing would never have tempted me. But I must have been like a starving rat—a rat ready to eat its own tail off. Diversion was the one thing I wanted. I was willing to pay any price for the timely anæsthesia of activity. I could no longer resist that inner and incessant ache for some opiate-like venture, for something to shake me out of my own thoughts.

For five long days of idleness I had been brooding over two strangely alternating figures. One was the girl of the Unknown Door; the other was the young woman who had appalled me with the pretence of a third arm. For five idle days disquieting scenes had haunted my brain. They kept driving all thought deeper and deeper inward, galling and fretting me with moods I could not fathom. They had become a hidden and persistent torture, as tangible as that of an ingrowing nail.

I had dipped into the bustle and movement of Broadway. Yet even that had not sufficed; it had left me still an outsider, a pariah, an idler. So I went back to my suit-case, with its neatly packed Outfit, went back to it as a frantic-minded sufferer might go back to his hypodermic. Some propulsion other than my own will seemed driving me once more down to the febrile ways of the Under Groove. I found myself starved for stir and excitement, dizzy with that most drunken of all intoxications, love of subterranean warfare. I couldn't help taking a high-dive back into the old-time pool of life, merely to relearn the freedom and buoyancy of it all.

And there that unlocked door had swung and dangled, just off the main current of the Avenue, like a fly in front of a tired and hungry trout. And there, forgetting my surroundings, I had waited and circled and back-finned until the moment seemed ripe. Then I made my dash.

It wasn't until I was actually inside the door that I stopped and listened, and, peering through the gloom to the right and then to the left, began reckoning on the risks I had taken. So far, though, everything seemed safe.

I tucked my skeleton-keys away out of sight. I next took off my gloves. Then I transferred my revolver from its padded hip-pocket to the pocket of my coat. Then, resting my heavy suit-case on a rug, I cautiously lifted out from among its wires and cells and instruments my little storage flashlight, no larger than a morocco-bound prayer-book. Then I groped my way forward, slowly, step by step.

It had been a pretty neat piece of work from the start. There had not been a blunder, a single false step. And there was still plenty of time before me. I was a little worried, nevertheless, at the fact that the entire front hallway was in darkness. That was not the usual order of things, even this early in the evening, for houses of this stamp. But it had one advantage. It would make my work easier.

I tried the first door or two, cautiously, merely to make sure of a possible retreat in case a servant passed my way. Remotely, from below-stairs, I could hear the drone of someone singing and what sounded like the occasional clatter of dishes.

The first two doors, I found, opened into quietude and darkness. Everything was as safe as a cellar. And in fifteen minutes, if I chose, I could be out and away from the house again.

Suddenly I was startled by a voice, almost at my elbow. It was a woman's voice, clear and cool and authoritative, and it sent a tingle of dread down my crouching body as I recoiled and wheeled and let my hand drop down to my coat-pocket.

"*I've been watching you ever since you came through that door!*" were the words that sounded out of the darkness before me. And I realised, from the calm and deliberate tones of that young woman's voice, that she likewise knew what I was and just why I was there.

II

I had no time, however, for further thought. A sudden light exploded on the darkness, almost as she spoke, and I knew that her fingers had fearlessly switched on the electrolier.

At the same moment, through the ache of light in my eyes, I saw the woman herself there before me. She stood close beside an open door, to the right of the wide stairway. She held nothing in her hands. And my first tangible thought was that she was a very foolish

85

young woman, for she was laughing a little. I could surmise that the ferociousness on my startled face, or the ridiculous back-crouch of my sudden fear, was enough to make anyone laugh. But I saw the smile slowly die out on her lips and her face touched with a quickly mounting bewilderment.

It was the girl of the Unknown Door. My blind burrowings had brought me into the Shaler household, face to face with the one woman I had always secretly dreaded to meet.

I thought I saw her startled lips frame an incredulous *"You?"* But not a sound came from them. She merely backed away, with her great searching eyes still on me, until the wall cut off all further retreat. It was not fear that caused the movement; it was more one of horror, of instinctive repulsion, of momentary recoil, until she had come to some new readjustment of things. My own fears, too, as she stood there still gazing at me with her white and impassive face, merged into a feeling of blind rage, of resentment at the scurvy trick that Fate had played me. I was helpless; I could think of nothing to say.

"I might have known!" she half-whispered.

"I'm sorry to frighten you!" I stammered out, at last, making a show of courteously removing my hat. The inadequacy of my beginning was only too evident.

"Pardon me, but you didn't!" retorted the girl, with much more spirit than I had expected. "You only—you only humiliated me!"

I could see her drop her hands to her side with what seemed a smile of self-pity. On second thoughts I took it to be one of disgust. Yet she still stood searching my face. There was something in her gaze that made it hard for me to look back at her. So I let my glance circle about, toward the street door. I could hear an involuntary sigh break from her studiously compressed lips.

"Oh!" she cried out, clenching her hands with a child-like little gesture of anger. I held up a finger, warning her to be silent. But it was unnecessary, for her rage seemed to pass away as quickly as it had come.

"You needn't be nervous," she said, in a moment, with her forced smile, "I'm not going to scream."

"Then we're only detaining each other!" I ventured, stepping back toward the door.

"We *are*!" she answered, with a decisiveness that brought me up sharp.

That foolish young woman never knew how near I came to seizing her and flinging her headforemost into a frond-draped Vilona palm-tub, as I stood there calculating my chances of getting away before she could recover and give an alarm. But she was wary and kept watching me, moment by moment. So I still hoped the old-time Chesterfieldian ruse would come to my help. I was vain enough to remember that once my presence at her side had not left her unimpressed. The memory of that episode, I knew, I had already outraged. But when it comes to a woman and her emotions, I had long since found out, you can never tell which way the cat is going to jump.

It was the girl's voice that brought me back to the predicament of the moment. Something crisp and peremptory about her tones made me more than ever afraid of her.

"Come inside, please," she said with a motion toward the room door.

There was nothing for me to do but go. She was not an ordinary young woman. And after all, it was much safer there than in the open hallway.

She was also a very discreet young person, for as I stepped softly in after her and closed the door she stood facing me, squarely, with her left hand half-carelessly clinging to the tasselled crimson bell-cord.

"Sit down, please," she said.

I placed my precious Outfit suit-case beside a club-chair and made myself comfortable. Then I succeeded in forcing a laugh. It was hard to do, but I felt it was time for it.

"You *are* a cool one!" was all she said.

"May I return the compliment?" I ventured. Once more she was looking over at me studiously, but this time almost in perplexity, I thought. We were in a luxurious room done in forest-green and white. The walls were flanked with low bookshelves, and here and there the gleam of a statuette or a bit of carved ivory touched the gloom with a sprinkling of highlights.

"So you are a burglar?" she ruminated aloud.

I was silent.

"A house-breaker? A thief of the streets?"

It was more a declaration than a question, but again the curt and businesslike tones of her voice left me floundering in sloughs of doubt.

"Let's put it I was dropping in for a cup of tea!" I parried. Women, I knew, were, more often than not, susceptible to the touch of gentility in a criminal, and my best plan would be to humour her and await my first chance of getting away. But she was still studying me, closely, debatingly.

"Are you in need of money?" she suddenly asked me. "Are you poor?"

"Aren't we getting a bit personal?" I equivocated, wondering what she was driving at. Then I noticed her hurried little hand-move of impatience. I also noticed, for the first time, the strange and undecipherable look of trouble that had crept into her eyes.

"But why do you ask me that?" I ventured.

Her eyes coasted the room with a gaze that astonished me, for it was a gaze of utter misery, of hopelessness and rebellion.

"Because you have broken into a house of thieves!" she cried.

III

The unhappiness of her face left me speechless for a moment. Then I echoed the word "Thieves?"

"Yes, thieves!" she answered, and I thought from the sudden heaving of her breast that she was going to burst into tears. She made a dab or two at her eyes with a bit of lace, but that was all. Then, with a little upthrust of each rounded shoulder, she seemed to pull herself together, rather proudly, and turned back to me with a second sudden change of manner. As she looked down at me she emitted a gasp and took a step toward my chair, with her lips parted.

Whatever she had willed to say was left unspoken, for at that moment there smote on our ears the sound of slow and solemn steps passing in the hallway without. Above these steps rose a thick and placid voice, chanting what must have been a coster song. It was, I surmised, nothing more than a bibulous footman or butler ascending the stairs. But the woman carefully switched off the light until the house was silent once more.

"I was hoping for a moment that you were in want—that you were miserably poor," she began again, looking at me with widening eyes.

It was my turn to shrug a shoulder: my spirits were rising.

"But, surely, if you could risk such things"—she moved her head in the direction of the street door—"for the mere sake of a little——"

She broke off, in her growing misery, as though uncertain of herself.

"Or *are* you just a sneak-thief with the soul of a sneak-thief?" she inappositely demanded of me.

"If I were *that*," I righteously retorted, "you'd have been throttled some time ago!"

She seemed to be pondering what I had just said.

"And we might never have come out through a certain door together!" I was shabby enough to remind her.

"I know!" she said weakly, wanly. But still again she pulled herself together. And again my hopes went down.

"You must listen to me!" she suddenly exclaimed. "I must tell you at once. Time is too precious for either of us to be beating around the bush like this! You're a man of intelligence—you've got brains. And you must have *one* kind of bravery, or you'd never be here!"

I bowed to her all too flattering denomination. She brushed my frivolities aside with an impatient hand. A sudden, more tragic look came creeping in about her meditative eyes.

"I've just decided—I've just been compelled to decide on something where I need help, now, to-night, at once! I need *your* help! I can't—no; I daren't do it alone!"

I took advantage of her moment of preoccupying excitement to rise from my chair. I still thought it safer nearer the street.

"Then why not explain a little more fully?" I asked, as a blind. She made one of her peremptory motions for me to reseat myself. This I did, with a sigh. Yet there was something almost companionable in her attitude as she sank limply into a chair before me. It reminded me of an earlier and happier scene. I noticed her look down at her little gold watch with a start of dismay.

"Oh, we've been losing time!" she cried, starting to her feet again. Then she wheeled on me almost triumphantly. "You've *got*

89

to do it! I can compel you to—I can make you choose that or the police!"

"I think I'd rather do it the other way!"

"Would you?" she asked, fired with a sudden hope.

"Perhaps, when I know what it is!"

"Then listen," she hurried on tragically. "Fifteen minutes ago I found out too much about you—now you must be told too much about me and mine! That will put us on common ground—it will be making it a case of honour between——"

"Thieves!" I finished for her.

"Yes—yes, it's that!" she gasped with a frightened look about the room. "I can't tell you everything now—I can only explain enough to make you see that what I have to do is not so mad as it seems!"

"Please go on," I said, as she came to a stop.

"I have a younger brother," she continued, with difficulty. "He has been in some terrible kind of gambling game with a man named Travis. This afternoon he went to his father's office. It was to borrow money, I think—he had been drinking. And when he was alone there for a few minutes he took—he *stole* thirty thousand dollars out of the vault!"

IV

I stood watching her while she struggled to gain her composure once more.

"I don't think he dreamed he was taking so much," she went on, unsteadily, but determinedly. "I don't think he quite knew what he was doing. He didn't mean to steal; he thought it could all be returned. He's only a boy—a poor, pampered, irresponsible boy! But every dollar, every penny of that money has to be put back!"

I bowed, comprehendingly, and once more waited for her.

"You see," she said, wringing her bit of lace, "this is the hard part of it. No one must know! It must be done before his father goes back to the bank to-night."

"To-night?" I interjected.

"Yes, to-night. He always goes back on steamer nights! He would never forgive him—he would be relentless! You see, it would mean his honour, his name—everything!"

She was in tears by this time, crying miserably, bitterly.

"Then why not have the young gentleman take it back himself?" I demanded.

"That's what makes it so hard—it's too late! It's impossible. The boy is not—I mean he's—he's not responsible—yet!"

I thought I understood.

"He was a thief. I myself had to be a thief to save him!" she sobbed. "And unless it's returned, every officer, every clerk in the company will know of it by ten o'clock to-morrow! And his father—all of us—have overlooked so much."

A slow and insidious wine seemed creeping and singing up through my veins as I stood there listening to her words.

"Oh, *can't* you see?" she said with a note of passionate appeal.

"Where is this vault?" I demanded.

"It's at the City International offices in Wall Street."

"How could we ever get into those offices?"

"It's not that—it's getting into them before father is there, before anything is known!"

"What time will he be there?" My businesslike tones seemed to calm and reassure her.

"He always goes to the University Club first—then he rides down in the touring-car. He would get there by nine, or a quarter after nine!"

"Then we're simply losing time here," I cried, glancing at my watch. "Have you a carriage?"

She stopped half-way to the door. "Oh, they must never guess—the brougham would be dangerous! We'll have to go in a motor-cab or a hansom!"

I caught up my hat and gloves and suit-case. I wished, at the moment, that heavy Outfit was at the bottom of the East River. But I daren't leave it behind. The woman was studying my face with strangely luminous and exalted eyes.

"Oh, you'll help me, won't you?" she cried as we slipped out of the darkened hallway into the quietness of the street. She had caught up a heavy silver fox throw-scarf and a glistening and gold-monogrammed patent-leather handbag as she went. "You *will* help me, won't you?" she repeated as we scurried on toward the street-corner where an electric cab stood beside the curb.

"To the finish!" I answered contentedly.

V

"But what am *I* to do in all this?" I asked, more doubtfully, as the cab-doors slammed shut and we went thumping and rattling toward the dull glow of light that showed us where Broadway lay. The freedom of the street again seemed to give me a new clearness of vision: I began to anticipate the awkward moments of the coming situation.

"There's just one thing," said the young woman at my side as she opened and groped through her handbag to make sure something was there. "The watchman!"

"But do you know there *is* a watchman?" I asked.

"Of course," she answered, almost tempted to smile at my innocence. "I've always known a great deal about the offices and things. I've always been interested in them and remembered what I've heard. Father and Uncle Cornelius, you see, often talk over the vaults and locks and fire-protection and all that, at home."

"But this watchman of ours—he interests me extremely."

"Yes, that's mostly why I needed you."

She looked at me with her bland and child-like ingenuousness. "You'll have to get him out of the way by some manner or means."

"You don't mean by force?"

"Oh, no; certainly not!" was her answer. I began to see how little she realized just what she was facing. It was only her utter solemnity that kept me from laughing, her femininely unimaginative obsession to shield and save her own. It was worth something, I inwardly concluded, to have a woman like that fighting for one.

"But, my dear young lady, are you aware of the fact that this watchman will be armed, and as ready to shoot you or me as to kill a fly?"

"But don't you understand—he'll never suspect—he must never see us!"

"Then how, in the very first place, do you intend making an entrance to the building itself?"

"Very simply! I have father's set of duplicates—his keys for everything except the vaults themselves!"

She was, after all, more or less a business man's daughter.

"But even then—the vault is the one thing you want!"

"But there again I have the combination. It's a permutation lock, you know. The time-locks aren't set steamer nights, as we call them, until father leaves for home."

Here, indeed, was a situation! She was more than ever worthy the name of a financier's daughter.

"Then, after all, we needn't worry or hurry."

"But don't you see, unless I get in there before those time-locks *are* set—even before father is there to set them—I'll never get in at all? No one could! Not even the whole board of directors themselves!"

"But how do you know? Why are you so sure of this?"

I had to confess to myself that this particular young woman was still a good deal of a puzzle to me.

"For the reason I've just told you. I've been listening to casual talk about such things ever since I was a child. I never thought, until to-day though, that what I knew would have to be made use of!"

"Couldn't you make it a little clearer for me—some of this talk you've picked up about the vault we're going to visit?"

"Father's office, as I said before, is in the International department. His vault is the biggest in the bank, I think. First there's a vault-cage that can be locked by electricity from any part of the building. The vault itself is a Medwin with a Kermiss burglar-proof door. Inside this door is the day-grate and then the teller's safes and the smaller compartments. The door is the tenon and groove kind, I think it's called. It's drill-proof and it's as thick, I remember, oh, as thick as your body! Then it's equipped with both the permutation and the chronometer locks. I mean by that there's a multiple combination and also a time-lock. It can be wound and adjusted at night for any time, say ten o'clock the next morning. Then, when the door is once locked, all New York City couldn't get it open before that time."

"Why couldn't it be dynamited?" I asked, for I still had certain empiric doubts about anything in the burglar-proof safe line.

"It could, of course, but it's built to resist explosive force, so that anybody trying to get in *that* way would have to use a charge big enough to wreck the entire building. And that would probably wreck the burglar as well. Then the vault itself is built on granite and concrete to prevent tunnelling. Above it, for the second vault-bed, are twenty-five layers of carburized steel alternating with malleable iron, all bolted together. I've heard Uncle Cornelius boast about that carburized steel for years. Then the door to each vault-chamber is fitted with a burglar-alarm and another automatic alarm set off by any contact with the inner surface of the vault. That, of course, can be easily switched off, as they have to do it every day during business hours. For instance, father wouldn't reset the alarms until he was leaving for the night—to save the risk of sending in an accidental call and having a patrol wagon full of police pounding down the doors. That really happened, once!"

"Go on," I requested, as she stopped, apparently at the memory of the episode.

"Then the vault chambers are so arranged they can be flooded with steam at a moment's notice. I always used to tell father *that* seemed cruel."

I did not relish the thought of possible death by steam heat myself.

"Each watchman," she went on, "is locked in wherever he belongs. He must stay there until he's relieved from duty in the morning. There's always an electrical recording-dial where he is; every half-hour he has to be there waiting to register. That's to show he's awake and watching."

"But what, especially, is kept in this vault?"

"Besides the smaller subdivisions the vault itself is divided into two parts by a steel door. One-half is the bullion chamber, the other half is for papers and things—stocks and bonds and treasury notes and all that sort of document. For instance, last week the *St. Paul* and the *Campania* together brought three million and a half of our stocks and bonds back from London."

"For this one vault?"

"Yes. When the ships arrive in New York these papers are unloaded by special porters of the steamship companies. They are nearly always in quarter-million lots, packed in tin boxes. They are taken straight to the International office and opened. Then the securities are examined, counted, and the endorsements inspected. After that they are stowed away in the vaults while the original borrower is notified and the loan 'pending transit' is at an end. Am I making it too *banky* and *Wall-Streety* for you to understand?"

"No; I think I follow you pretty closely." My bewilderment was due to the colossal figures, in which imagination itself seemed to be engulfed.

"That's why it's so carefully watched and guarded and audited. And can't you see, that's why the taking of this money would start such an uproar? It would be the first stain on their record. Even father himself couldn't put things straight again, once it got known!"

"But have you once realised the risk, the danger, you are going to face? Have you stopped to think of the possible sacrifice you're going to make just to stop the discovery of a theft already committed?"

"It's worth the sacrifice, I think," she answered, a little proudly, perhaps a little quixotically.

I could see by her face that I was confronting a young woman unschooled in the ways of the actual world—a wilful, arbitrary, determined girl, who, having once made up her mind to a course of action, followed that preconceived path to a bitter end. I had, of course, always disliked working with women. With them, as I have already said, you can never tell which way the cat is going to jump. And there's always the danger, too, of letting feeling blind the eyes of judgment. I even sat back, as our cab came to a stop at the curb, and asked myself if already my better judgment had not been warped and blinded, if I had not embarked on a fantastic fool's errand, a wild-goose chase leading into nothing but danger?

VI

A feeling of walking through phantasmal unrealities, of some ludicrous nightmare projected into the sanities of a waking world, took possession of me as I stood watching the fur-clad figure of the woman as she stooped before the great barred bank doors. There was something amazing in the mere thought that her slender gloved fingers, with a quiet and silent little movement or two, were defying and throwing open such solemn and ponderous portals.

"We must go quietly," she whispered as the doors closed on us again. I found myself creeping forward between partitions of bevelled plate-glass set in mahogany panels, past glimmering brass-grated windows and wickets behind which the dim night-lights burned, past doors that stood as ominous and threatening as the port-holes of a man-of-war cleared for action.

I felt myself clutched suddenly by the elbow and drawn into one of these mysterious rooms.

"Sssh!" whispered the girl at my side.

For, firm and steady, out of the distance, came the tramp of feet. It was the watchman making his rounds. He was following the direction we had taken, westward, toward the vault chambers. He would pass the door behind which we crouched.

I could hear the woman's breath, quick and short, as she stooped there at my side. Then she did not even breathe, it seemed, for the tramping feet were upon us, opposite us, then safely past us. The gloved fingers fell from my arm. I heard the ghost of a sigh escape the girl's lips. The tramping feet died away in the distance.

She peered out past the door, cautiously. She even crept farther down the carpeted corridor. Then she flew back to me, noiselessly. She was behaving much better than I had expected.

"Quick!" she gasped under her breath. "*Now* is our time! This is our chance!"

I was in doubt as to what she meant. Then she whispered: "But take off your shoes!"

I heard the crisp rustle of silk and linen. The woman was deliberately tearing her underskirt to pieces, deftly knotting a strip or two of it into one compact ball, from which trailed two heavy ruffles of the torn linen.

"He's waiting at the recorder to make his half-hourly report," she whispered in my ear. "The moment his arm goes up to write on the dial you must get him, in some way, from behind!"

The woman was obsessed.

"Then what?" I demanded.

"Don't kill him—be sure not to kill him!"

"But supposing he kills *me*?"

"He can't, if you only do everything right!"

She was an Amazon now, panting for victory at almost any cost, blind to everything but the battle confronting her. "When he's down, safe, force this into his mouth and tie the ends at the back of his neck. Then get him back into this room."

"And then?" I asked.

96

"Then tie him securely. See, here's a Mission couch. Tie him to that, full length, hands and feet. Then the door can be locked and the way will be clear for us!"

It was dangerous work. But now, I felt, it had to be neck or nothing. And it had its tang of peril, its zest of uncertainty. But as I crept noiselessly and cautiously down the corridor and beheld the shadowy figure waiting before the recording-dial I firmly settled one thing in my mind. Now that I was committed to this hare-brained business, now that I was in it up to the ears, now that I was facing my risks and taking my crazy chances, I would make my visit to that bank-vault worth while.

VII

I was panting and wet with sweat when I crept from the room and the waiting woman quickly locked the door. I carried away both of the watchman's guns, stowing them down in my suit-case. I felt more at ease knowing they were out of his reach, although I had left him bound and trussed like a braising capon. I intended to make no mistake about being interfered with from that quarter.

"Now, quick!" said the Amazon at my side, leading me from the corridor into a carpeted room and out by still another door into a second corridor. Each door, I noticed she carefully closed and locked after her, as she had found it. This was a line of procedure somewhat in opposition to the professional's, who always likes to know his way of retreat is open. But at no move or moment did she lose her self-possession. She scarcely realised, I knew, the enormity of her undertaking, the danger of her surroundings. She still felt herself to be the banker's carelessly indulged daughter, I concluded, long accustomed to invading that financial holy of holies at her own sweet will. It took my breath away to think that I was having my pace set for me by this slip of a girl. Yet still again I turned and studied her face. And still again I was reminded of the fact that my companion was at heart more a woman than a girl, that she had known life and tasted of its bitterness.

I looked up to find myself in a richly furnished private office, with rosewood desks and chairs. A large window, curtained and heavily barred, convinced me the room was an outside one.

97

The woman suddenly turned to me with a little gasp of terror, of disappointment, of perplexity.

"Look!" she whispered. "This is the door that leads to the vault-chamber. But, see—there's a burglar-alarm attached to it—it would bring a dozen men from the First and Second Precinct Stations!"

I stood on a chair and examined the door carefully. Then I dismounted, opened my suit-case, and with a pair of lineman's nippers pried away a little of the moulding that ran along the lintel woodwork. This exposed the wires. Then I followed my usual procedure of scraping away the insulation and bringing the two wires together with a short "jumper" of Number 18 from my Outfit case. In other words, I shortened that alarm-circuit by the length of the upper part of the door, just as a surgeon shortens an artery (without material loss of the vital current it carries) at the end of an amputated limb. I thought I detected a momentary look of admiration in the girl's eyes, as she watched me insert my "jumper" and replace the moulding. But when I turned to her she was already fitting the key to the lock. I was a means to an end, an instrument to her, that night, and nothing more.

A moment later we were in the vault-chamber itself, face to face with the great "Medwin," with its impregnable Kermiss portal and its background bulwarks of iron and steel and concrete. I realised, as I gazed at it, how the struggle of the safe-builder had been a struggle to defy the burglar, fighting him field by field, meeting each new tool with some new medium of resistance, each new force with some new machinery of defiance.

The woman had already flung off her silver fox throw-scarf and tossed her handbag on a desk beside it. She was breathing short and hard by this time, and I could see the feverish restlessness in her eyes. But even then there seemed no touch of doubt or anxiety in her manner.

She walked straight over to the face of the great vault door, taking out a slip of paper as she went. I could hear the muffled click of the metal as she turned and spun and adjusted the polished nickel dials of the permutation locks.

Then she wheeled to me with a sudden start.

"Listen!" she said.

I listened, but heard nothing.

"Look back, quick, and see if everything is safe!"

I slipped into the other room and then on to the hall-door, listening. It was well I did so!

Quickly I darted back to her, with a little cry of alarm, to warn her in time.

For, out of the distance, somewhere, I had once more heard the sound of approaching footsteps.

I caught only a glimpse of the startled woman as she disappeared into the vault. I saw the great door swing to behind her. But there was no time to explain, to warn her. I swept the room with one frenzied look, caught up my telltale suit-case and sprang for the window with the drawn curtains.

I found myself in a veritable cage—there was just room for my body between the massive iron bars of the bulging window-grating and the two sashes themselves. Once outside, with the window closed again and my body pressed against the cold plate-glass, I stood there waiting, listening, feeling that the worst had happened.

I looked aimlessly and despairingly about me as I waited. My window overhung an inner quadrangle of office buildings. Here and there a lighted window opposite me showed where some sedentary worker still toiled over his books. Above me I could see a star or two, cold and hard in the high square of sky. Angling on a wooden block, studded with insulators, just above my head, at the upper right-hand corner of the window, ran the wires of some power or light circuit. Then I noticed nothing more, for my attention went back to the room within.

The steps had drawn nearer. I could hear them loud and clear now on the polished floor, then low and muffled on the office rug. This was followed by a second or two of silence. Then came the snap of a switch as the drop-light on the rosewood desk was turned on; then, again, the firm, quick steps as they crossed and recrossed the rug, the whine of a chair-castor, the meditative and preoccupied thrumming of finger-ends on a desk-edge. Then came the rattle of a ring of keys, the thud of an open desk. Sifting through the crack between the window-sashes I could sniff the mellow fragrance of cigar smoke.

It could be no one else than the girl's own father. What she had most dreaded had actually taken place. Shaler himself had returned to the office.

Then I listened again, for once more I could hear the heavy footsteps crossing the room. Then came silence, and again the sound of an opening door. A still longer pause was broken by the sound of the footsteps again and the sudden shrill of a telephone-bell. Then came the quick, guttural call for a number I could not overhear.

"Is that you, Everson?" at last sounded the voice at the 'phone. "This is Shaler speaking, from the office—Shaler. Can you tell me just why Number Three was left with the combination off?—What?—I say it was *closed*, but not *locked*—yes, Number Three—never mind, now.—No; report to me in the morning at ten.—That's useless; that would do no good.—No, it's folly coming down.—I say I've set it already.—Can't you hear me?—I say *I've set the time-lock myself*!"

VIII

My first impulse was to spring through the window, pane and all. That, I realised on more sober second thoughts, would only be taking foolish risks. But there was not a moment, not a second, to be lost. The man in the room before me had locked and imprisoned his own daughter in an air-tight vault, had hermetically sealed her in a chamber of steel and concrete that could be nothing but her death-chamber before even one inch of that hardened metal could be chiselled away. If the words he had just spoken were true, that imprisoning vault, once held shut with its great chronometer locks, could hold out all New York until the time appointed for its release. Until those relentless wheels, as implacable and slow as Fate itself, had turned their predestined number of revolutions, until the predetermined number of hours had ticked and dragged and measured themselves out, no power of heaven or earth, no agency, either illicit or legitimate, could throw open that great steel door.

Then across the foreground of bewildered consciousness flashed a sudden thought. It came and went like a glint of lightning. But it was enough, for it had brought with it, like the detonation after the stroke itself, a hollow and far-off echo of hope.

It caused me to fling up the window-sash, without hesitation now, and leap into the room. I was over the startled banker, as he leaned beside an open drawer, even before he could stand upright.

He gasped, looking at me as though I had been an apparition. It was only for a moment that my descent stung him into helplessness. He wheeled about with one loud shout for the watchman. Then I caught his hand as it darted out to a drawer in front of him. I knew that drawer held a revolver.

"What does this mean?" he cried, struggling to get as far as an electric alarm-button behind the desk.

"It means you've just locked a woman in that vault!" I cried, tearing him back from his desk.

"Who are you?" he cried again, vacuously.

"Quick!" I gasped, knocking his hand aside as it went out to catch up the telephone-receiver, "or it'll be too late!"

He thought he was face to face with a madman.

"The vault!" I cried. "You've locked it!"

"I did!" he answered, struggling to free himself from my insane clutch on his shoulder.

"Then you've trapped and locked a woman inside it! You're suffocating a woman to death—and *she's your own daughter*!"

"You're a fool!" he gasped. "You're crazy!" He still struggled to get to the telephone.

I held him back, despairing. Then I saw my salvation.

"Look!" I cried. My eye had caught sight of the silver fox throw-scarf. "Whose furs are those?"

Beside them lay the gold-initialled handbag. "And whose pocket-book is that—quick?" I demanded insanely. No wonder he thought me a madman.

He leaped for them and caught them up in his hand, his staring eyes wide with incredulity.

"Margaret's! My daughter's! Here!"

"Quick, man, don't waste time!" I warned him.

"You're crazy! You're a madman!"

"Aren't those hers?" I panted. "Can't you believe me?"

"What d'you mean by saying—What's *she* in this building for?" He was tearing at the door by this time.

"I don't know—I can't argue about it now—she's *there*, and that's enough! She's in that vault, and in half an hour, I tell you, she'll be as dead as a canned sardine if you don't come to your senses and listen to me!"

"You're crazy—you're a madman!" was all he kept saying.

"Do you or do you not want to save that woman's life?"

I was desperate now, for I had already roughly computed the air-space in that hermetically sealed death-trap. I realised that after thirty minutes, perhaps even less, nothing could save the woman. I could even imagine that death—the fighting and panting for breath, the gradual suffocation and collapse, the terror and agony of it all.

"Is this a new kind of yegg game?" he mocked.

"Save that woman!" I all but screamed.

"Is it money you want?"

My look of scorn must have convinced him. I had decided to knock him down in one more minute and go on with my work in my own way as he lay there.

"No one could get into that vault!" he insisted.

"She knew the combination, I tell you. She'd often heard you talking it over. She got your key duplicates. She stood in the inside chamber when you closed the door. Good Heavens, there are your own key duplicates."

"But why, man, *why*?"

"Get her out of there before she's dead and she'll be able to tell you!"

"Why isn't this some crook's game to get into that vault? How do I know you're not lying?"

"You found that door open—couldn't I have *been in* if that's what I was after?" I thrust my Colt into his hand; I was getting beyond the point of arguing.

"Here, shoot me through if the girl's not in that safe! What more do you want? And I tell you again every second you wait you're bringing her nearer death—you're burying her deeper every breath you waste!"

I wheeled and peered at the door. My plan was already plain to my own mind. The door was of the "stepped edge" type, with tenon and groove to resist both wedges and explosives. Then I sprang for my suit-case.

"Wait!" gasped the banker. He swung round to the great safe door and knocked on it with the butt of the gun. Then he listened, his face chalk-coloured. There was no sound, and again he tapped with the gun-end, holding his ear close to the enamelled metal.

Faintly, from within, came the sound of an answering tap. The sweat beaded the man's face.

"This is awful—this is incredible—it's——"

I was busy lifting out the Outfit—the Outfit I had been cursing for three long hours.

"But what are we going to do? That time-lock is set! It's too late! Nothing but a ton of dynamite could open that vault!"

I knew he would wake up in time. I was too busy to console him. I let him do the worrying from that second forward.

"What are we going to do?" he repeated weakly.

"Listen!" I cried out to him as I plunged feverishly into my work. "This is our only hope—our only chance. Two days ago I submitted a process—my own particular process—to the engineers of the Harahan Building. They'd driven interlocking steel piles down through the clay to the rock."

"Yes—yes, go on!"

"The face of that bed-rock was uneven and these interlocked girders had to be cut off level. I got a plan for burning those steel piles off—burning 'em off with electricity. I found that by tapping one of the street mains and reducing the power with a transformer, bringing it down to a voltage of about fifty, and an amperage of about five hundred—it was an alternating current, remember—I could burn and fuse away each girder, between the two poles, in eight minutes' time; I could cut 'em off as clean as a cross-cut saws a log."

"But what's that to us?" cried the frenzied man.

"It's this—there, at that window, thank merciful Heaven, we have a power wire, a live power wire, man—the very wire we need! I've here an emergency kit—this 'step-down' transformer will tame and regulate that current I'm going to tap, will make it our slave. This end of the wire, see, I'm attaching to the safe hinge. At the end of the other—here, quick, get a fire-axe and knock that letter-press loose—I've got to have the cast-iron plate out of it for a shield! Quick, man, quick!"

He did as I ordered dazedly.

"This other wire," I rattled madly on, "will end in an electrode—so. The moment the power's on—and two minutes now will do it—it will be applied to the safe door somewhere here above the lock apparatus. Then that current is going to eat and gnaw and burrow and corrode its way through."

I was only dimly conscious of his drawn and haggard face following me as I darted about the safe-front, rattling on with my explanations as I worked.

"Hand me that emergency switch! I'd say the body of that vault must be interlapped with gypsum or silicate or asbestos for the sake of the fire-proofing. That'll keep the heat purely local. So, in half an hour, in less, even, we'll have that lock burned away and the door open!"

I snatched up my lineman's gloves and pliers.

"Keep tapping on that door," I told him. "Let the girl know we're still here! For the love of God, don't let her think we've left her!"

He did as I ordered, without outward protest, though I could see doubt and incredulity still written on his colourless face.

"But that safe's burglar-proof! It's hopeless! The door is impregnable! It's made of the hardest drill-proof chromium steel!"

I laughed down at him deliriously as I worked.

"Burglar-proof! No safe was ever built that the right burglar couldn't get into if he worked the right way! Burglar-proof? Pooh! And you say it's drill-proof—that it's the hardest of chromium steel? Good—for the harder that steel the easier we'll make it fuse!"

He followed me blankly as I leaped back into the room. He watched me, each move I made, stumbling back, every minute or two, to tap reassuringly on the great steel door, giving vent to a relieved gasp at the answering knock. He brought me his fur motor-coat and goggles, at my order, while I worked over the transformer. He pounded out a tin letter-box for a second and wider body-shield against the heat glare. I'd already quietly cut out his telephone connection on the pretext of needing the wire.

Then I was ready. And it had taken me considerably less time than it would take to describe it.

IX

I clapped on the goggles and pulled on the thick fur coat, protecting and shielding my face and body as best I could with the letter-press plate. Then I faced the great door and snapped shut my emergency switch.

There was a blinding flash, a leap and hiss of flame, and the smell of scorched paint, of burning enamel, filled the room. The imponderable and mysterious force I had stolen from the wire was already at work.

A little area of dark rose appeared in the gray-black of the scorched steel. It deepened and brightened to a dull glow, to a cherry glow. Across the entire face of the door it spread and ran like a living gulf of fire. It grew paler and brighter, wider and fiercer. I stood there dripping, choked with the fumes of burning fur, as the fire mounted to a blinding incandescence. I could feel my shield growing warmer and warmer. I could see the sleeve of my coat begin to smoulder and drop away in cinders. My eyes ached excruciatingly; it was like staring broadside into a noonday sun.

But still my electrode kept its place, still I watched and directed that tearing and eviscerating and raging current, burning across its sullen river-bed of steel.

"Quick, now!" I called to the man behind me. "Put on your motor-gloves and stand ready! Have your fire-axe!"

He did as I bade him.

"See, it's going! It's honeycombed! It's as rotten as cheese! It's as soft as soap!" I cried like a madman.

"But it's too late!" groaned the man. "It's too late!"

"See! there go the lock-tumblers!" I cried. We could hear them fall, the muffled concussion of metals, within the works.

I swung off the current and caught the waiting axe from his hand. I was almost blind at the moment. I could see only the still incandescent glow of the metal that was scorching my skin, singeing my eyebrows, burning the very hair off my head.

But I crushed in on the corroded, rotted metal, I cut into the slag and cinders. And the axe-head went through the devitalised tissue as though it had been chalk, with a little whistle of air that told me the shell of the safe itself had been penetrated.

I used the axe, then, somewhat after the fashion of a fireman's hook, tearing and wrenching at the heavy lock-mechanism. Something fell away at each wrench, at each stroke. I could hear the man at my shoulder panting, quick and wheezily. Suddenly he began to shout, past my ear, into the cavity before him.

For I had cut through to the very vault itself.

No answer came to his shout. Together we tore and pulled at the burned-out lock-bar releases, wrenching them, one by one, from their sockets. Fragments of the heated metal had fallen about on the wooden flooring, smouldering and eating down into the varnished boards until they seemed like the pitted timbers about a blacksmith's anvil. A rug had caught fire; the thick smoke from it added to the purgatorial disorder of the place.

But we fought like madmen there before that great charred door, for even with the bolts drawn back we found it annealed and cemented, by the heat, in each flange of the stepped edges, glued to the body of the vault itself.

We fought and wrenched at it until the ponderous thing of ruin slowly yielded and swung back on its charred and rotted hinge.

I tore my goggles off, flung away the burned fur coat, and staggered back to the wall, faint and dizzy. There I leaned, for a moment or two, panting for breath, vaguely and foolishly wondering if I was going to be blinded for life.

As sight came back to my dazed eyes I could dimly make out the figure of the other man, in the body of the vault, stooping over the figure of the woman. Then I could hear his cry:

"She's fainted—she's only fainted!"

He was half-lifting, half-dragging, her huddled weight out into the air.

"I tell you she's alive—she's breathing!" he exulted.

I felt weak and faint and sick myself.

I called to him, asking where I could find water; but he did not answer. Then I remembered. I was nothing to him, to either of them. I had turned my trick: there was nothing further asked of me. I belonged to the streets, to the ways of the Under Groove.

I could hear the man call to her, frenziedly, tenderly, as I staggered toward the door. There was nothing to do, now, but to leave him with his own. I had known my hour, and it was over.

I stumbled dizzily out into the corridor. Once there I ran like a pelted and homeless hound down those quiet and empty halls until I came to the street door. I wrenched it open with my pocket-jimmy. Then I rounded the corner and hurried on, automatically, without sense of direction or destination.

CHAPTER SIX
THE ADVENTURE OF THE EMERALD PENDANT

I

I waited until the lamp-lit street was empty, clear to the corner of Madison Avenue. Then I swung about and walked casually down into the area. Under the shadow of the wide, stone house-steps opened the double doors leading into the basement.

The first of these was really more a gate than a door. It was made of wrought-iron rods above, and of fantastically perforated sheet iron below. It served as a guard for the inner door, which was of wood, and opened into the little entry. From this entry, leading into the actual basement of the house, opened still another door.

The sheet-iron guard no longer troubled me. I took out my keys as off-handed as though I were a head servant returning from shopping, threw back the lock, and calmly opened barrier number one. The fitting of that key, however, had already consumed much time and energy. I had first used a "skeleton blank" for taking a ward impression. The key-bit had been dipped into melted wax. It had then been inserted carefully in the lock and slowly turned. The wards that held the lock-tumblers in place had registered themselves on the soft wax, showing me just what to leave and what to cut away when it came to a matter of filing.

It was practically the same procedure with the inner door of wood. The key for that had also been duly fitted and filed and made ready. But that was as far as I had been able to go.

Once safely inside the entry I carefully locked both doors behind me. Then I felt about under the brownstone fluting of the house-steps and cautiously exposed what I suspected was a burglar-alarm circuit. The wires of this circuit I scraped clean, for a few inches, and then brought them together at the exposed points, leaving the circuit shortened but still "closed." The wire beyond the junction-point I promptly cut away. Taking from my pocket a third key-blank, carefully wrapped in tissue paper, I inserted the wax-covered bit in the lock of the still obstructing house-door, and turned it slowly but firmly against the resisting wards. Then I caught up my slender little key-file again and cut away the serrated line imprinted on the wax.

In ten minutes I had the door open and had stepped inside. It was a house in which I had begun to take an almost proprietary interest. I felt peculiarly and contentedly at home, in spite of the fact that it was my first visit across that threshold. For days, now, that house had meant much more to me than a mere mask of brownstone. It had taken on mysterious possibilities. It had piqued and challenged my curiosity. I had come to know the team of well-matched bays that day by day drew up in front of it. I was familiar with the limousine that swerved and shuddered up to the curb under its steps. I knew its motor-car and its phaeton-victoria, its impassive coachman and its footman and maids.

But, most of all, I knew its mistress, the young and autocratic beauty of the fine sables, the ebullient and airily poised Mrs. Gaillard-Goodwin, who had kept the society reporters of the evening papers in copy for a season or two. I could likewise claim a more or less intimate acquaintance with her jewels, though it would be wrong to say that I had at any time found these jewels more interesting than their wearer. A few words at the Madison Avenue corner drug-store, an occasional discreet surveillance of the house, a patient and consistent perusal of those columns in which are recorded the comings and goings of fashionable city folk, a casual observation of her friends and her frivolities, an equally casual investigation of the habits and business interests of her husband, to say nothing of a quite accidental discovery or two—these had equipped me with a knowledge which might have startled the owners of that huge and silent house through which I was now cautiously making my way,—and while doing so they had served to make life once more endurable, to milestone with incident a lonely and ghost-like road that seemed to begin nowhere and end nowhere.

There were many things about my life that I could not answer. Yet there were many things about the life of my involuntary host that were now quite well known to me. I was aware, for instance, that the gentleman in question was denominated Thomas Gaillard-Goodwin, of the Goodwin and Cobalt Operating Syndicate, that among other things he was the president of the Alaska and Littoral Hydraulic Mining Company, that only the day before he had hurried back to New York from Washington. There, I knew, he had been busy making final arrangements for the Kamchatka Coast mining concessions from the Russian Government. To this end, obviously, both he and his discreetly audacious young wife had striven to make a certain Count Rezanova's visit in New York a conciliatingly agreeable one, and the effort, as I was left open to judge from a veiled hint in a weekly purveyor of circuitously penned society scandal, on one side at least, had not gone unappreciated.

Such trivialities as that, however, lay beyond my province. It had been of more interest to me to make sure that Gaillard-Goodwin, the same day of his return to New York, took a train for Boston, to attend a directors' meeting there. His wife had motored in from their country place at Rye-on-the-Sound, apparently to meet him. She had brought none of the servants, excepting a French maid. The town house had been peremptorily closed and boarded up the afternoon of the mine-owner's departure for Boston, and the motor-car had carried Mrs. Gaillard-Goodwin promptly back to the Rye place. Only the maid had been left behind, to essay an afternoon of shopping.

Before this maid had begun her afternoon of shopping, however, she had seen fit, immediately after her mistress' husband had given orders for the closing and barricading of the town house, to despatch a certain telegram. Strangely enough, I happened to be in the little district telegraph office, puzzling over the wording of an imaginary message of my own, when the young operator stopped eating a beef-tongue sandwich long enough to send the maid's "rush" despatch out over the wire.

It was addressed to Mrs. Thomas Gaillard-Goodwin, Miramar Hall, Rye-on-the-Sound, and, as it was ticked off in the hurrying dots and dashes, I read:

"The note and emerald pendant have been locked in the bedroom coin-safe."

And it was, on the whole, merely to find out a little more about that enigmatic pendant and coin-safe that I was making my way into a house whose blank front had stood before me so uninviting, yet so challenging and alluring.

Now that I was inside, I found the house somewhat different from what I had expected. I stumbled from no elephant-limbed Mission lumber into gilded anachronisms of Louis-Quinze rooms. I found no *nouveau-riche* theatricalities of design and decoration. Instead, there was something about that blithely solemn house that mysteriously appealed to me, from the electroliers of pale-tinted tulip-buds to its morocco-upholstered, automatic elevator with mother-of-pearl signal buttons. There was a discreet sense of luxury, of machinery subjugated to mood, of careless and light-hearted well-being, in its very silence and spaciousness, in its ample chairs and serviceable open fires, in its soft confusion of colours and unruffling inevitability of furniture arrangement.

As far as I could see, nothing of importance had been packed away. I found no dispiriting striped ticking on the chair-backs. Neither the gas nor the electricity had been turned off. An open fire of hickory logs awaited a match in the library. Companionably low bookshelves suggested evenings of quiet reading in the wide-armed leather lounging-chairs. On a wide-topped buffet still stood decanters, a small humidor, a gold-banded liqueur flask.

But it was the repose of the place that most appealed to me. It made my feverish and shiftless street life seem suddenly mean and foolish and squalid. Most people who are down, or have never been up, have their incongruous hankerings after grandeur, I suppose. But most people are satisfied to take their grandeur second-handed, by mooning over it in the pages of smart-set fiction, or blinking at it over Empire Theatre footlights. That canned variety had never appealed to me. I always wanted to get hip-deep into the real thing; as Dinney used to put it, I had to "take it hot off the griddle!"

I looked about me meditatively. With the exercise of ordinary precaution, I felt, I could have many a pleasurable hour before me. The house might remain closed for a week, for a month, even. In the mean time, until the return of the woman of the sables, I would be able to come and go at my own sweet will.

So I made my way up through the quiet rooms, looking casually, yet appreciatively, about me as I went. Everything on both the first and second floors seemed orderly and undisturbed, as I let my storage flashlight circle and play about the polished surfaces and the subdued colours and the unexpected recesses. There was nothing to dispel the all-pervading atmosphere of home-like comfort; it seemed to creep through the house like perfume through a garden.

I ascended to the third floor, almost reluctantly. It was made up, I judged, of what would be the main sleeping-rooms of the house. So it was somewhere here that the coin-safe would be found.

I began my search methodically and with a singularly disengaged mind, opening the first door at the front end of the hall. I found myself in a woman's boudoir. My pocket searchlight quickly showed it to be a truly feminine chamber, of pale rose and gold, with a Watteau box-couch and ivory-tinted rattan chairs. Between the two front windows stood a large pier-glass. On a slender-legged desk, of the same pale ivory shade, rested an electric reading-lamp. Beside it glimmered the burnished metal of a telephone transmitter. Not far from this, again, was a dressing-table glinting with a scattering of toilet articles in silver and cut glass. A subtle odour of cosmetic or perfumery of some sort pervaded the place.

A second door, opposite the hall, opened into a bedroom, also of pale rose and gold. From the rear of this bedroom opened still two more doors. One led into what proved to be a white-tiled bathroom, the other into what appeared to be a small dressing-room. At the end of this narrow dressing-room I was confronted by yet another door.

I turned the handle of this door carefully. It was unlocked, but it refused to swing back. My effort to open it, guarded as it was, brought what I took to be a heavy portière down on my startled head. But it was not this falling portière that left me suddenly rooted to the spot where I stood. For out of the darkness of that inner bedroom my ears were suddenly assailed by the loud sound of snoring. Some one was asleep in the bed before me. Then, as I stood there listening, I knew that I was hearing not the sound of one's man's snoring, but of two.

That trumpeting and wheezing of contented slumber was unbroken; it rose through the darkness, rhythmical, dissonant, continuous, brute-like in its placidity.

I quietly stooped and lifted the fallen portière to one side. As I did so I discovered the thing at my feet to be not a curtain, but a heavy woollen blanket. Why it had shrouded the doorway I could not tell, but my sensations, as I took a step or two deeper into the room, could not have been much different had I been invading the lair of sleeping tigers.

In fact, as I stood there, trying to pierce the darkness that surrounded me, something heavy and animal-like in the very atmosphere made me still again think of a tiger lair. I could see nothing. Not a ray of light showed in the room. But every nerve in my body warned me that I was in the presence of life, of menacing and combative and ferine life.

I had my storage lantern with me, and one press of a thumb might have pricked the whole bubble of mystery. But only a fool would flash a light in a sleeping man's face. Yet by some means or other I still had to find out who and what were those sleeping figures before me. The sheer, inexplicable puzzle of the situation seemed to increase the longer I stood there waiting and listening.

It even prompted me to take a noiseless step or two forward, so that I stood almost at the foot of the bed from which purred and boomed out that enigmatic and immoderate duet of sound. I began to sniff the odour of stale cigar smoke. Drifting after it came the unmistakable fumes of alcohol. I dropped down on my hands and knees, intending to crawl forward until I reached the side of the bed. As I did so my groping fingers came in contact with an empty bottle. It rolled and clicked against a second bottle, leaving me there, holding my breath, for a terrible moment or two of suspense.

A sound broke through the darkness, but it did not come from the sleepers in front of me. I swung about sharply, for in the pink-and-gold room I had just left I had heard the quick opening and closing of a door. A moment later came the click of an electric-light switch, and the blackness of the half-opened door behind me grew into a faintly luminous oblong. My retreat had been cut off. Somebody had entered the room behind me.

III

My first rational and conscious movement was toward the door. I was on the point of promptly closing it, of shutting myself in with the ferine pair on the bed, when my relieved ear caught the sound of a bell ring. That curt and hurried tinkle, I knew, came from the transmitter of the desk-telephone in the boudoir beyond the pink-and-gold bedroom.

Then came a second or two of silence, and the hurried call for a number. It was a woman's voice that spoke. The moment I heard that voice I knew it belonged to Mrs. Gaillard-Goodwin: to the mistress of the house into which I had forced my way.

I crept to the end of the narrow dressing-room, and listened. The first few hurried words had escaped me, but as I stood there waiting I told myself that I was hearing quite enough.

"Yes, it's the same safe we had the trouble with before, Mr. Kerwin," the woman at the 'phone was saying. "Yes, the coin-safe, the one you sent your man up about, two months ago. . . . But we don't *know* the combination. . . . Yes, it's urgent. . . . Two hours? . . . Yes, I *could* wait. . . . Oh, from Brooklyn! That's different, isn't it? . . . Then couldn't I get a locksmith, or something, nearer here? . . . An expert, just for that? . . . Well, I'll wait. . . . If it's that late, tell him to give four rings, so we'll know. . . . Yes, it really *is* too bad. . . . Thank you. . . . Good-night!"

Before the last faint vibration of that 'phone bell had died away I had tested and weighed and decided on my plan of action. To wait a reasonable length of time and then make my entrance as the safe expert from Brooklyn was out of the question. Anything I intended to do would have to be done before that particular expert sounded his four rings on the front-door electric bell. It would also have to be done, I felt, before the unknown sleepers in the room behind me had awakened. I no longer pondered who and what they were. All I knew was that they were asleep and that from the room where they lay some second door must lead to the hall without.

I darted back through the door of the unlighted bedroom and closed it silently behind me. I would have locked it, but there was no key. The sleepers still snored there, uninterrupted, placid, indifferent. I felt blindly along the walls, in the darkness, carefully coasting each obstructing piece of furniture, until my fingers came in contact with the soft folds of what I knew to be a silk comforter, hung flat against the side of the room. Under this comforter, strangely enough, I found the door. It refused to open as I turned the knob. But the key was still in the lock, and a guarded turn of the wrist permitted me to squeeze out to comparative freedom. I reached in for the key, on second thoughts, and locked the door from the outside.

I could see the light from the open door of the woman's boudoir fall across the front of the hallway. I still had a fighting chance, for that light implied the mistress of the house was still there. The open door further assured me that nothing had as yet aroused her suspicion.

I sped down the dark and silent stairs as quietly as possible. My first intention had been to go clear to the street door and there hurriedly sound the electric bell. But that, I saw would be a waste of time, for any such ring would never be heard on the third floor of the house. So at the bottom of the second stairway I wheeled suddenly about, and tramped noisily up to the third floor again. The light still shone from the open door across the front hallway. But no move or sound of interrogation came from within at my approach. This was disconcerting; but it was too late to draw back.

"Is anything wrong here?" I demanded authoritatively even before I swung about into the square of the lighted room.

Still there was no answer to my question as I stood there in the doorway, accustoming my eyes to the glare of the light.

But there, directly before me, I saw the woman, with her back to the huge pier-glass. One hand rested on the edge of her ivory desk, the other was pressed close against her panting breast. She was swaying back and forth, weakly, as she stood there. Her lips were parted, foolishly; her face was the colour of paper. Her eyes, wide and fixed with some sudden terror, were gazing through the half-opened door toward the narrow dressing-room that opened into the bedroom still farther to the rear of the house. Through the momentary quietness, above the quick breathing of the woman, I could still hear the low and animal-like *vibrato* of the two sleepers.

Involuntarily I circled about and looked in the direction of the woman's fixed stare. Each door stood open, and I could see clear through to the room from which I had so recently escaped. That room, I saw as I peered into it, was now flooded with the unmuffled white light of its electric lamps.

"What's wrong here?" I demanded, turning back to the room where she stood. She continued to sway back and forth in front of the pier-glass, without so much as looking at me. The woman, I could see, was beside herself with terror.

"Who are you?" her lips said indifferently, as she still faced the half-open door and the lighted room beyond it.

114

"I found your street door left open. I thought there might be something amiss inside."

She turned slowly and looked at me as though she had just awakened out of a sleep. She struggled to draw herself together, with a futile little movement of her hand across her dazed brow.

"I'm a Holmes' special officer," I explained. "Do you want help? Is there anything wrong here?"

"There is!" she gasped, peering into the open door again.

"But what?" I asked, taking out my Colt from its carefully padded hip pocket.

"*Look in that room!*" she whispered faintly, sinking into one of the ivory-tinted chairs.

IV

I turned and strode toward the open bedroom with a peremptory show of indifference. But my pulse was far from sluggish as I stopped in the doorway and peered inside.

Before me lay the high-ceilinged room, tinted a pale blue, and now flooded with the clear white light of the electrics. On a massive brass bed that stood in the centre of the room sprawled two ludicrously dishevelled figures.

Never before had I seen two figures more out of keeping with their surroundings. One man, unkempt, carrot-headed, cadaverous, lay partly wrapped in an eider-down comfortable of brocaded satin. His great rough boots lay on the white sheet beside him. Protruding from the flowered satin folds that covered him showed one red foot, in a tattered woollen sock. And all the while he lolled and wheezed and slept there, blissfully oblivious of everything about him.

Another more gigantic figure lay sprawled out close beside him on the white mattress. One dark and hairy arm, thrown carelessly above his head, drooped across the burnished rods of the bedstead. His face was of a dull crimson hue. His gorilla-like wrists protruded from the red silk sleeves of a dressing gown much too small for him. His great heaving and snoring body, crowned with a saturnine sort of placidity, stretched, uncouth and incongruous, from the top to the bottom of the bed, coarsened by the fine linen against which it stood out with the clearness of a cameo. There was something

115

unspeakably loathsome about the black stubble of his unshaved face, about the thick, loose-hung lips, now wide apart.

Yet one close glance at that figure had shown me who and what it was. The sleeping hulk on the bed before me was "Scranton" Sammy, the one-time "gay cat" of the "Pennsy" yegg gang. The other sleeper, the carrot-headed figure, I could not place. But it took no second scrutiny to show me that I was face to face with a couple of the lightest-handed criminals outside of Sing Sing; and I was not without a passing sense of gratitude at the thought of having stumbled upon them in that comatose and helpless condition.

My first reactionary feeling, as I let my gaze wander from the figures on the bed to the scene close about them, was almost one of humour. For the two intruding yeggs, careless of consequences, had obviously been regaling themselves on the good things which the house had offered. An empty decanter or two, bottle after bottle of vintage wine, the remnants of some potted meat, a box of sweet biscuits, an empty magnum of champagne, a jar of brandied peaches, plainly showed me how ample and irresponsible their orgy had been. The children of the open had been revelling in the long-dreamed-of luxuries of wealth. The temptations of that quiet and empty house had been too strong for them. They had fallen victims of sensation, even as I had done.

The thought made me wince. The sensations of which I walked the slave were of a higher order than theirs, perhaps. Yet I knew they all led to the same end. I looked still further about the room. The two windows at the back were blanketed, just as the two doors had been. Even as I puzzled over the mystery of this my eye fell on the key to the whole enigma.

A square, fumed-oak cabinet, ornamented with roughly cut brass hinges, stood in the southeast corner of the room. It was surmounted by what appeared to be a writing-desk, with small oak drawers and pigeonholes. It was, I saw, an ungainly piece of furniture, designed to hide away, when the oak-doors across its face were closed, a low-grade house-safe in a lower-grade effort at ornamentation.

Its doors, however, were not closed at the present moment. One heavy brass hinge, in fact, had been wrenched away in forcing them open. At last I began to understand the meaning of the blanketed doors and windows. It was a quiet prelude, as a rule, to a noisy entertainment with which I was more or less familiar. It was a performance which usually claimed for its *dénouement* a shattered safe front.

The face of the joint around the inner steel door of the safe before me had been carefully filled with putty, with the exception of one small space at the bottom and another at the top. On a level with the lower space that had been left unsealed had been puttied a piece of window-glass a few inches square. On this still lay a scattering of some finely powdered explosive. In front of the safe my eyes fell on a small air-pump, with a rubber suction-disk attached to it. Near by lay what I knew to be a fuse and "timer."

The situation grew still clearer to me. The two prowling yeggs had made note of the fact that the house was a deserted one. They had broken in, presumably by way of the roof, had discovered the safe, and had begun their campaign of attack. While one worthy had attached his suction-cup to the upper crack of the safe door and worked his air-pump, the other had fed his finely powdered explosive along the piece of glass adjusted to the lower crack. By this ingenious device they had, presumably, sucked in between the tenons and grooves of the safe door enough powder to blow it off its hinges.

Knowing it would be safe to detonate their explosive only in the dead of night, they had obviously whiled away their time by a further inspection of the house. Thus waiting and lounging about, they had surrendered to the sirenic call of the wine-cellar, had eaten and drunk their fill, and, with the *sangfroid* of utter intoxication, had gone calmly and blissfully to bed in the very room where they had laid their mine.

Even as I looked back at them, there seemed something symbolic in their brute-like slumber, something typical and tragic in their lack of comprehension while strange and momentous currents were stirring so close about them.

They were not fitted for the paths of pure adventure they had elected to follow. They made my mind flash back, even in that moment of hurried inspection, to poor old Dinney, my one-time pal. Dinney, after his haul from a St. Louis bridge-builder's house, had ached to adorn himself in that unhappy gentleman's dress suit. He surrendered to this incongruous hunger for gentility, at last—and went to a vaudeville matinée, at three o'clock in the afternoon, in all his glory of white shirt-front. That innocent vanity had cost Dinney ten months of his freedom, through coming face to face with an officer who knew more of social procedure than did poor Dinney himself.

I was brought back to the crisis before me, at a bound, by a metallic click, followed by the sudden tinkle of the telephone-bell, in the room behind me. It was too late now, I knew, for any outside interference.

Switching off the lights, I swung the door of the blue room shut, and darted back to where the woman sat at her ivory desk, with the receiver in her hand.

I was just in time. I noticed that she had grown more self-possessed, that she now had more control of herself. There was an air of sudden determination in her glance, as I almost flung myself between her and the 'phone.

"What is that for?" I whispered hurriedly.

"I'm telephoning for the police, for help!" was her answer.

"But what can the police do?"

"Do? They can protect me from those brutes!" she cried out. I held up a warning finger for silence. Then I took the receiver from her hand and hung it on the hook.

She sat there watching me, without speaking, while I muffled the call-bell in the palm of my hand, and continued to do so until Central, exasperated, grew tired of ringing.

"*I* am here to protect you!" I warned her. "And whatever is done will have to be done most carefully!"

Her terror of the situation seemed about to return to her.

"What do you mean?"

I looked toward the closed door that led into the blue room.

"I mean that the men in that room are two of the most audacious and most ruthless criminals in all New York!"

"Oh!" she said, under her breath. She made it almost a moan.

"We are safe enough for a little while," I assured her. "But first you must explain things to me. Is this house empty? I mean, where are your servants?"

"Quite empty," she answered. "The servants are all at Rye. The house has been closed."

"Then you came here to-night by the merest accident?" I asked.

"I came unexpectedly," she answered.

"Why, please?" I demanded.

The faintest tinge of colour showed in the pale oval of her cheeks.

"It's a not unnatural prerogative, is it, to come into one's own house?" she replied. I realised the rebuke. I also realised that she was shrinking away from me as I stood over her. Yet I did this merely that our voices might not carry beyond the room.

The woman did not appreciate her actual predicament. A touch of a bell, or a word to a footman, had always brought her orderly service, on the one hand, or adequate protection, on the other. For once in her career she was facing life without its veneer. She was finding herself engulfed in certain primordial conditions where her code would always go unrecognised and unknown.

She started to rise from her chair, half-impatiently. But I forced her back into it. My movement of authority seemed to irritate her even beyond the bounds of precaution.

"What are you doing here?" she cried out imperiously.

Again I held up a warning finger for silence.

"First let me explain something to you. Do you understand why two men are in that particular room of your house?"

"No," she answered, watching me narrowly.

"Then let me make it clear to you. As you know, there is a coin-safe in that room, hidden away in some sort of oak cabinet. They have forced that cabinet open, and sealed the safe door up with putty. Then they have applied an air-pump to the upper crack, to exhaust the pressure on the inside of the safe. They left a small crack in the bottom, and as the air rushed in it carried enough finely powdered potassium picrate to blow that safe door to smithereens at the touch of a match!"

"But——" she began. I stopped her with a movement of the hand.

"They have made everything ready. But they knew an explosion would not be safe, until midnight, at least. That explains why they are still there!"

"But what could they want from that coin-safe?" she asked uneasily. Some momentary restraint of manner, some faint shadow of passing embarrassment, crept over her.

"I think I can explain that!" I told her.

Her lips framed an almost inarticulate "Why?"

The step was a bold one, but I had blocked out my line of advance and had to follow it.

"Because the same purpose that brought those two yeggmen into this house also brought you here!"

I knew the shot had struck home, the moment it had been delivered. The woman drew back in her chair, wide-eyed and gasping. It was not anger and denial I saw on her face. It was more wonder and bewilderment.

"You don't know what you are saying!" she murmured, steadying herself and studying my face. The incongruous consciousness that she was a very beautiful woman, even through her pallor and lines of fatigue, took possession of me as I sat peering back into her immobile and guarded eyes. She was beginning to be a little afraid of me after all.

"Those men are thieves—are criminals!" she began.

"Precisely," I interrupted. "They are criminals who took their lives in their hands the moment they broke into this house! And for that very reason they would put a bullet through you or me, if we stood between them and their safety, as quick as they'd put their hands into a cash-box!"

Still again she was studying my face, narrowly, intently. She was pondering, apparently, just how much I knew of her life and movements. I was beginning to feel we were both doing a great deal of foolish beating about the mint-patch. And time, I knew, was flying.

"Listen to me," I said, with a decisiveness of tone that held her attention even against her will. "You know, and I know, that in the coin-safe in that next room is locked a note and an emerald pendant!"

A gasp broke from her lips, involuntarily.

"We also know," I continued evenly, "that it is vital to your happiness and peace of mind (let's put it) that this note and this emerald pendant should fall into your hands, and into no one else's!"

She started up from her chair, with a movement toward the blue room.

"You *know* these men!" she cried with sudden conviction. I felt like gagging her on the spot.

"Madam, lower your voice," I warned her in a whisper, "or even *I* can't get you out of this mess!"

I motioned her back to her chair.

"We've no time for nonsense like this. As an officer, I know these men are yeggmen, and I know what they stand for!"

"Then you *are* an officer?" she interrupted.

"As I told you, I'm a Holmes' special patrolman," I retorted.

"Then why are you not in uniform?" she promptly demanded.

"Madam, I'm not a *watchman*!" I evaded, with all the dignity at my command. "I don't wear a gray helmet and sit up watching back stoops!"

"Well, go on!" she said, a little wearily and also a little imperiously.

"Those men in that room have started to break into your husband's coin-safe. In that safe are certain things for which you yourself came to this house to-night, alone!"

"Why should you think that?" she parried.

"I don't think it—I know it!" was my answer.

Again she rose from her chair.

"Then that safe is open! It's been broken into already!" she flung out at me defiantly.

My only answer was to lead her to the closed door. There, after listening for a moment or two, I turned the knob and switched on the lights.

The two loutish figures still snored there, sprawled out on the white bed. They did not make an attractive picture. What suddenly disconcerted me was the discovery that one figure had turned in its sleep since I had last seen it. At any moment, now, I might have other forces to deal with.

The woman's eyes swept the room, slowly, dazedly, shrinkingly, from the litter of empty wine bottles to the draped windows, from the brutal faces to the coin-safe in the corner. It was at the safe she looked longest. Then I motioned for her to go, and quietly turned off the lights. I also withdrew the key from the inside of the door, as we retreated, and locked it after me.

Once back in the room of pink and gold, we stood confronting each other for a moment of unbroken silence.

121

"What is it you want of me?" she said at last, in a tone of tacit surrender.

"I've got to know, once for all, just why you want that pendant!"

"But why should I tell you this?" she asked after a pause.

"Can't you see you may as well tell me quietly here as have to explain everything to a sergeant at the police station?" I argued.

"There are things about it that *can't* be explained!"

"Those are not the things I have to know!" I assured her.

"Then what must you know?"

"Why you want that pendant!" I reiterated.

She took a deep breath.

"Simply because it belongs to Count Rezanova," was her deliberate answer.

VI

I made a quick effort to conceal my surprise. Here was a cropper indeed!

"Then what is it doing in your husband's safe?"

"Because my husband *put* it there!"

"But why he put it there is what I want to know!"

"That involves so many things," she complained wearily.

"Then perhaps it would be well to begin with the Kamchatka Coast mining concession!" I suggested.

Her eyes widened at this.

"And you compel me to explain?" she still equivocated.

"Circumstances compel you to explain, madam!"

Again she took one of her deep breaths.

"This is all I know," she began hurriedly. "My husband has been moving heaven and earth to get those coast mining concessions you spoke of. Count Rezanova came as a special envoy from the Russian Government for the arrangement of final terms between the company and his Minister. Tom—my husband—explained to me that Rezanova had a good deal of influence. He said it would pay us to be as agreeable to the count as possible."

She stopped, and looked over at me a little indignantly.

"Oh, it's all so ridiculous," she complained, "and yet so close to being tragic!"

"From which I am to imply that what you intended as the merest amenities of hospitality were perhaps construed into something less impersonal?"

I knew it was not easy for her, so I did what I could to smooth the way as we went.

"I had to do the usual things, of course—a dinner-party or two, a few nights at the Metropolitan, a little motoring, an occasional cup of tea here at home with him."

"And?" I said, as she stopped meditatively.

"I don't think the count really understands America yet. . . . He has such absurdly continental ideas about women, I mean. . . . You see, he's a foreigner, and our freedom seems so inexplicable to him!"

"But the pendant?" I said.

"As I intended to say, he rather presumed on his privileges. He sent me a note, a very poetic and ridiculous note, which, of course, was promptly torn up. But he must have taken my silence of indignation for something else. He found out that I had hurried in from Rye—almost as he had suggested. But it was, of course, to meet my husband on his way back from Washington."

"And he?" I prompted, to fill in the sudden silence.

"Rezanova thought it was to meet *him*, I'm afraid. At any rate, when I found my husband had to go on to Boston, I went scurrying home to Rye. Before Tom left the house a second note and, apparently, a pendant of emeralds—they were dug, I think, from Rezanova's own mine—came here for me!"

"Had you explained this—er—mistake of Rezanova's to your husband?"

"My husband is rather quick-tempered at times—he does things that he's sorry for afterward. The Kamchatka concessions meant a great deal to him!"

"But how does the coin-safe come in?" I demanded.

"My French maid, who sometimes seems to be unnecessarily discreet, promptly told Tom the package was a reset bracelet of mine that had been sent back from the jewellers with the bill. He was in the front hall, behind her, when they came. So my husband flung them into his coin-safe, and locked it, for he'd given orders to have the house shut up. I hurried into town, at once, as soon as my maid got home and explained a telegram she had sent me."

"But it's lucky you *were* brought back here," I assured her.

She was silent for a moment, deep in thought.

"You'll telephone for your reserves?" she said at last.

"That's too late," I answered. "And you've already implied you don't want the story in the morning papers!"

"That pendant has *got* to go back to its owner," she cried in desperation.

"Do you know the safe combination?"

"No—but I've 'phoned for the lock expert. He should be here any time now!"

"But we can't sit here with our hands in our laps, waiting for that man! What's more, it's no longer necessary."

"I don't quite follow you."

"Wait!" I whispered, running to the door of the blue room, to make sure nothing had as yet disturbed the sleepers. For a new line of advance had suddenly opened itself to me.

Everything was quiet within. As I hurried back to the lighted room, I saw the woman sitting before her desk, bending over a morocco-bound address-book stamped in gold. It was only too plain that she was about to call for some number written in that book.

"Listen: is that the bell?" I asked from the hall-door. The ruse was effective.

She ran to the balustrade at the head of the stairs, and leaned out over the darkness, listening. I was, of course, wrong in my impression as to the door-bell, but before the puzzled woman had returned to the lighted room I had cut the telephone wire.

My move had not been a mistaken one. I was making a feint of listening for the sound of snoring, beyond the closed door, when she hurried back into the room. But, the moment she was there, she sat down at her desk and impatiently caught up the receiver.

"Even this 'phone is cut off!" she whispered with rising alarm.

"But we have no time for *that*!" I warned her. "If we're going to do anything, we've got to do it in the next ten minutes!"

"I'm quite ready," she answered.

Then she wheeled about and peered at me for one thoughtful second. "Every door would have to be open downstairs before we could hear the bell ring, this far away."

That was quite true.

"Wait here," she whispered, crossing the room.

I could hear the sound of her feet and the rustle of her garments as she hurried down the polished hardwood stairs, lower and lower, until the darkness below swallowed her up. It suddenly occurred to me that it would be safer to get rid of my file and skeleton-keys in case things came to a pinch.

I darted back to the door of the blue room and cautiously opened it. The duet of the two sleepers continued unbroken and undisturbed. I groped my way toward the bed and quietly dropped my keys down between the two sleepers. A muffled chink of metal smiting on metal fell on my ear.

I stooped nearer, and reached in over the snoring, insensate, wine-soaked body. My exploring fingers were rewarded by coming in contact with a heavy bulldog six-shooter. I dropped it into my pocket gratefully, and crept for the door and closed it after me.

VII

I was quietly waiting in the middle of the outer room when the woman returned. She faced me, in an attitude of waiting, a look of mild interrogation in her eyes.

"What I'm going to do is simple, but dangerous," I began, taking out the drunken yeggman's bulldog revolver. As I had expected, her face suddenly sobered at the sight of the firearm.

"You take this gun, and stand here at the door!"

"But what are *you* to do?" she whispered, almost in my ear.

"I'm simply going to wheel the coin-safe across the bedroom and out through this door!"

The simplicity of the thing seemed to make her forget her fears. She stood at the door, without moving, as I crept in and switched on the lights. She watched me clear a passage across the littered room. She waited on guard as I pushed and wheeled the heavy oak cabinet that held the coin-safe slowly across the carpeted floor. Once, as the ponderous thing of oak and iron slewed against the jamb of the door, she caught her breath, with a feminine little gesture of warning. I reached back and promptly switched out the lights as she did so, for one of the men on the bed had mumbled brokenly in his sleep and rolled over restlessly.

Once through the door, I locked and closed it behind me. Then I worked the safe slowly forward, through the narrow dressing-room and into the room of pink and gold. That left two closed doors between us and the sleepers.

I next wheeled the safe about, so that it faced the bare side-wall of the room. Then I took the fuse—it seemed a small specimen of the Bickford type, wound with overlapping tape—and worked its tapered end well into the door joint, above the square of glass where the powder had been sucked into every mortise and groove and aperture.

My next move was to muffle the front of the safe with a heavy woollen steamer-rug and a couple of velvet cushions caught up from a Morris-chair. Then I took out a match, and motioned for the waiting woman.

"There will be at least thirty seconds between the time you light this fuse and the time of the detonation," I went on.

She nodded.

"The moment the flame of your match touches the fuse we must bolt."

She drew back as I struck the match.

"*You* must light it!" I commanded, with a motion toward the fuse.

"I had rather you would," she pleaded, drawing still farther away from me.

"I prefer that safe-owners should open their own safes," I explained to her. The match, in the meantime, had burnt out. I lighted another, and thrust it into her fingers.

"But it frightens me. I'm——"

She did not finish, for even before she had realised it the flame had come in contact with the fuse powder.

We scurried out into the hallway and down the wide stairs, like two frightened rabbits. We groped and ran and dodged, side by side, until, at the head of the first stairway, the low and muffled rumble of the detonation above smote on our ears.

I started back up the stairs, guardedly, with the woman at my heels.

"Is that all?" she whispered incredulously.

I nodded: the explosion had been much milder than I myself had expected.

But it had effected its purpose. That much I knew the moment I hurried into the smoke-filled room and began stamping the fire from the smouldering steamer-rug, which had been tossed into the corner. I motioned for the woman to open a window, and then sprang for the safe.

Its massive steel door, buckled and twisted and warped, had been torn clear away from its hinge sockets. It hung on one bent lock bar, like a bird's broken and trailing wing. Three metal shelves divided the exposed interior of the safe into four sections. Staring at me out of the disorder of the top shelf lay a sealed envelope and a small, flat, cream-kid box stamped in gold. In that box, I surmised, was the emerald pendant.

I had it in my hands and open before the woman could reach me from the window. But she stopped, with a little cry, as the light fell on the cluster of jewels against their pale satin background.

Each stone was a demantoid—a sister to the diamond itself. But, above the lustre and polish of that sister stone, it had the rarer beauty of colour. Each stone, with the exception of the centre one, which was a violet-tinged *rubino di rocca*, or Syrian garnet cut *en cabochon*, was of a beautiful green, too dark to be a true *hyacinth*, too deficient in yellow to be called a *jacinta la bella*. But each was that rarest of stones, a Bobrowska garnet, or, as it is more often called, the Uralian emerald.

I was startled back to reality by the woman tearing open the note, and by her gasp of indignation as her eye ran through its few lines. I suddenly remembered as I saw her there, that I had not yet made sure of my escape. And a moment later she was holding out her hand for the pendant.

"Wait!" I said, suddenly catching at her arm. Even beyond my pretence of fright I almost imagined I heard a faint splintering of wood. I saw that the woman was looking at me sceptically. So I stood upright behind the safe, and peered dramatically toward the door.

A cold chill, a tremor that was neither acting nor imagination, ran up and down my backbone as I did so.

For there, covertly watching us from the shadow of the doorway, stood the carrot-headed yeggman. He was still in his stocking-feet. From his left hand hung a pocket-jimmy. In his unsteady right hand he held a huge Colt revolver.

The fool was drunk still, unquestionably drunk, or he would never have taken such risks. From the room behind him I heard the call of a gruff voice, and the tinkle of falling glass. I caught at the woman, as I did so, and dragged her down behind the wrecked safe. The drunken fool might fire at any moment.

"Come out o' that!" exulted the maniac. I motioned for the woman to give me her bulldog gun. But she held it back determinedly. There was not a second to lose. My first impulse was to risk it and jump for the man. And being the first I decided it was the best.

But when I did jump, it was not toward him, but toward the electric-light switch in the wall not six feet away.

I dropped flat down on the floor as the light went out with a click. Darkness enveloped the room. I lay there, scarcely breathing, waiting for him to shoot, tugging at my own revolver, hidden away in its padded hip-pocket. But even his drunken brain recoiled at the menace of that sudden darkness. Instead of the thunder of his Colt I heard the pad of a hand on a wooden door, the soft whine of a hinge, and then the patter of unsteady yet hurrying footsteps, followed by the clink of rolling bottles on the blue-room floor.

He had gone.

VIII

A full minute dragged itself away. I rose to my feet with the utmost caution. The darkness that had concealed one man's flight could also conceal mine. The moment had arrived when discretion was indeed the better part of valour. I turned and began to grope my way noiselessly out toward the hall. As I did so my ear caught the faint and far-away ringing of a bell, followed by the quick thud of a closing door, far below us. Yet it was not four rings that the bell had sounded.

"Turn on the lights!" said the woman's voice with startling clearness and decision. I continued making my way out, until I heard the quick rustle of her skirts. I saw her with one hand on the switch as the room flowered into sudden brilliance.

"One moment, please!" she said, circling between me and the door.

"What is it?" I asked with forced calmness.

"You know what it is!" she answered.

"We can't let that man get away!" I blustered.

128

"There are other things that must not get away!" She still carried the bulldog revolver in her hand.

I essayed a Chesterfieldian bow, which was intended to imply that I was completely at her service.

"It's merely the pendant!" she said, confronting me. I stood there wondering what had given rise to this new note of assured authority. Then I deliberately dropped the kid case into my inner breast-pocket.

It was too late for quibbling. I was thinking of that bell-ring and door-thud below-stairs. Our duo might be interrupted now, at any moment.

"You shall have this pendant, madam, the moment I have ascertained these stones have been duly appraised by the Treasury Department!"

"That's an absolute lie!" she said, quietly.

Her right hand had come up on a level with my breast.

"Why do you say that?" I demanded.

"Because your first word to me in this house was a lie!"

"Madam!" I protested.

"You said you found my door ajar. When I came through that door I locked it with a chain lock!"

"The area door, madam," I began. But she cut me off short.

"They, too, were locked—all three of them. I tried them with my own hand!"

She suddenly wheeled about.

"This way, please!" she called aloud, and her full, high soprano rang through the quiet house. I could make out the sound of what seemed to be deliberate yet hesitating steps on the stairway below as she did so.

The steps were approaching the door. Yet as I reached down into my inner breast-pocket I let my fingers play about the hidden jewel-case, as though still reluctant to part with it. Something in the woman's eyes, however, warned me that any further equivocation would be dangerous. I dropped the gold-stamped case into her outstretched hand.

"*That is Rezanova*," she said a little grimly, in answer to my look of interrogation toward the hall.

"Rezanova?"

"Yes! You cut my wire, so I 'phoned for him, from downstairs."

Even as she spoke a wide-shouldered, white-browed, black imperialled foreigner of military bearing suddenly blocked the doorway. He was gloved, and in one hand he held an immaculate silk hat.

"You sent for me?" he asked in his suave, deep-toned, foreign barytone. I disliked the assurance and polished insolence in his eyes from the first.

"Yes, I did!" said the woman crisply. "This emerald pendant belongs to you. I wish to return it here, now, at once!"

I stepped to the door of the blue room, unobserved, as she thrust the kid-covered jewel-case into his startled hand. Had I been less hurried and harried in spirit I should have taken off my hat to that woman, as an expression of my admiration for her. And the man with the black imperial I hated more than ever, as I saw the momentary equivocal shrug of his condoning shoulders.

"They are *yours*!" repeated the woman, emphatically, with an almost contemptuous gesture toward the case in his hand.

At my last glance this strange pair were peering at each other, combatively, belligerently.

During the silence that followed their wordless contention of glances, I found the two blankets that had been tied together and left at the open window by the escaped yeggs.

"But, madam," said the voice of the Russian in suave amazement, as I swung out into the night, "*the case is empty!*"

There was another moment of silence. What the woman said I never knew. But, before vaulting a back fence and scrambling through the open basement of a half-built steel apartment house, I carefully wrapped the pendant in my handkerchief, for the minutest scratch or defacement of gems so matchless would have been an unspeakable misfortune!

IX

It was the next morning at daybreak that what then seemed the most foolish and inexplicable impulse of my life came to me. I tried to fight down this impulse with all the strength of my erratic and unstable will, for I knew it to be a contradiction of every law and rule of my Under Groove career. I fretted over it and struggled with it resentfully, through my gray and exacting hours of afterthought, when I should have been quietly and contentedly sleeping. But it was like trying to club a dog into a strange kennel. And in the end I surrendered. I let my grip on realities relax. Yet as I felt myself ebbing down that stream of impulse, I turned about, with a sudden ache of apprehension, and demanded of my inner soul if I was indeed losing my nerve, if my old clear-headed judgment of things could at last be leaving me.

Yet all the while I tried to console myself with the thought that I had won enough in winning my contest of pure wit against wit. My triumph had been in the battle, and not in the bays: in the race, and not the reward. This bauble that I had carried away was not the thing I had fought for. It was the fight itself—that was the only thing that counted. It was a pendant of rare enough Bobrowska garnets to the outward eye; yet in reality it was a standard torn from a courageous enemy and carried from a battlefield that was already tempting me with a lighter-flying ensign of victory. I kept telling myself that the thing was something above and beyond mere thief's swag. And as I kept telling myself this I also kept wondering what the girl of the Unknown Door would have said about it all.

That was how and why I surrendered. I had always hated to eat crow; but I surrendered. After still another hour of troubled thought I let Destiny take care of itself. I did what would surely have made poor old Dinney's back-hair stand up with astonishment. I carefully and deliberately wrapped the pendant in tissue paper and along with a written line or two sealed it in a plain manilla envelope. My written line or two read: "These stones belong to Mrs. Thomas Gaillard-Goodwin, of Miramar Hall, Rye-on-the-Sound, and by returning them to her I think you may be helping someone who has needed your help."

Then I made myself presentable for the street and directed my steps toward one of those earthy-smelling Broadway florist-shops that always reminded me of funerals. In this shop I buried my manilla envelope among an armful of American Beauties with straight green stalks as long as my leg, and stood by until I saw them boxed and directed to Margaret Shaler.

I wanted her to know. Just why I wanted her to know I could not explain, any more than I could explain the madness that had made me part with my hard-earned loot. I was, after all, being a good deal of a fool. And the whole thing, I felt, would have made old Dinney swear like a trooper!

CHAPTER SEVEN
THE ADVENTURE OF THE TRAVIS *COUP*

I

It had been a bad piece of business, from the first. The house itself had seemed inviting enough, with its ridiculous glass-doored American basement. My method of entrance had been above reproach, and the way had seemed clear, right up to the second-story bedroom, where I knew the bond vault to be.

But some vague new disgust with myself made me reckless. I had never dreamed that I should be a backslider into the ranks of the sentimentalists, a mush of smug concessions. More and more it exasperated me to think that a passing mood of remorse could drive me mincingly into a florist's shop and a parade of my half-baked virtues. It made me long for a dip into the old ways again, to wash away these sticky syrups of emotionalism. It sent me headlong back into the grim uncertainties of the Under Groove, ready to jump at the first chance of adventure.

That, I suppose, is why I made my advance without the usual preliminary reconnaissance. That was why I wandered into a place I had not previously deciphered.

I had already arrived, it is true, at a few conclusions, but I had never dreamed that the golf-playing, placid-eyed old banker who owned the house could be anything of an insomniac. Nor had I expected the old termagant to come at me, with my Colt staring him in the face. And, once I had him subdued and tied and trussed down on the bed, I had scarcely counted on the pertinacious old bulldog's working one hand free while I was busy over his vault door. Nor did I notice his finger on the mother-of-pearl push button beside him until I heard the sudden clang of the bell, away below-stairs, and then the call and answer of frightened voices.

The old fellow's daughter was in the room even before I had awakened to my danger. She was unarmed, luckily, but she fought and scratched like a wildcat. So I flung her bodily on the bed and muffled her and her screaming up in the blankets.

Before I got to the bedroom door I found myself face to face with the butler. He was a mutton-chopped, small-eyed Englishman, fat-handed, and only half-dressed. But he was stalwart enough, and full of grit. I had to fight it out with him all the way downstairs. Even at the street door he made a lunge to get my head in chancery, so I settled him with a ludicrous left-hander between his well-padded floating ribs.

But in the meantime the girl had got to the front window, screaming like a calliope, screaming until a policeman's whistle sounded from the Madison Avenue corner, and a bluecoat came up the block on the double quick. I had only time to bolt down the step and swing westward toward Fifth Avenue, with the bluecoat twenty yards behind me. I went like the wind, as I heard his shout, for I knew that any moment then, he would fire.

I heard the bullet "ping" over my head as I vaulted the stone wall of Central Park. Once over that wall, I raced on through the shrubbery until I was out of breath. Then I came to a stop, waiting and peering about me. I was safe enough for the time being. But in fifteen minutes, I knew, there would be an ever-tightening cordon about that entire park. My only plan would be to lie low until morning; then I could let the daytime stream of life that flowed back and forth catch me up and carry me out to freedom once more.

I began to feel very much at my ease. I had, it is true, six hundred acres to wander about in, and as they had been set apart for the precise purpose to which I was putting them, I decided to make the most of the situation. Having regained my breath, I sought out a more or less secluded park bench and sniffed appreciatively at the fresh smell of green grass and leaves. I even sank back and looked up at the sky, where the stars shone down from the high-arching heavens, calm and far away and inscrutable. But it was too much for me. The silence and immensity that blinked down at me seemed to leave me heart-sick and homeless and lonesome. It started me up and moving again. I went on and on, always keeping to the shrubbery and the shadows, working my way more and more southward. A chirp or two from a drowsy bird made me stop and look around. To the east, beyond the serrated line of the Fifth Avenue house-tops, a low streak of dull gray was slowly turning to pearl, and from pearl to pink. It was daylight coming on.

I decided to drop back to thicker shrubbery, where I could sit and smoke in comfort. So I crossed a loose-earthed bridle path, and then a carriage drive as smooth as asphalt, and pushed my way in through a clump of bushes. I crept on, noiselessly, to where I had caught sight of one end of a green-painted bench.

Then I came to a sudden halt, held there by the unexpected sight that met my eyes.

On the far end of the bench before me sat a young man, leaning forward, his elbows resting on his knees, his hands fallen dispiritedly between them. His attitude, as I watched him, was one of blank and hopeless despair. Then he slowly lifted his head and looked down at an envelope across which he had apparently scrawled a few words. This envelope he slowly put in his breast-pocket. As he did so I could see his face; it was colourless and lean, despairing and deep-lined. Then he peered through the shrubbery, deliberately, at the tree-tops, at the lightening sky, as though taking one last, comprehensive look at life.

I could see the cords on his lean side-face harden, and his right hand go down to his side-pocket. When he raised it again it held a little burnished, silver-mounted revolver. He peered at the thing vacantly, for a second or two. Then he shut his eyes. I could see him gradually raise his right arm until the silver-plated barrel almost touched the side of his head, just under his hat-brim. Then, and then only, did the necessity for immediate action come home to me. I sprang toward the wicked little plaything of steel and silver even before he could turn and look up.

The blow of my hand on his was so sharp that the revolver, spinning through the air, carromed off the bench-end into the bushes.

The man looked at me, dazed and speechless, his face heavy with the terrors of the brink over which he had been peering. Then his utter bewilderment gave way to an incongruous and slowly mounting rage.

"Damn you!" he gasped weakly.

I stooped and picked up the mother-of-pearl trinket.

"You keep out o' this!" he cried. "Keep away from me!"

He started up, and as he stood before me I saw that he was a young man—perhaps not more than twenty-one or twenty-two.

"Sit down," I told him. I pulled him down to the seat beside me. He struggled to get away, but I held him there.

"This is *my* affair!" he cried. He was trembling and shaking, now, as though a congestive chill had crept over him.

"So it seems! But you're going to tell me a little about it, first."

My grip on his arm did not relax.

"Who are you?" he demanded, still struggling to wrest himself from my clutch.

"*You've* got to answer precisely the same question first," I told him.

He stopped tugging to get away, and sat back, as though exhausted. His unstable glance went out to the wider circle of the city about us.

"What's the use of it, anyway?" he mumbled. I had asked much the same question, more than once, in my moments of idleness. It was a question that always sent me diving back into life, to drug my brain with some new anæsthetic of activity.

"The use of it?" I argued with him, nevertheless—"the use of it? Why, it's Life man, *Life!* It's playing the game as it comes—it's watching the great old gamble, whether we lose the stakes or not—it's just for the glory of going on!"

"I can't go on," he whispered. And then, to my utter astonishment, he started to sob and shake, like a woman. He was down and undone; he was a wreck, with broken nerves; he was, after all, only the shell and husk of a man.

"But why are you doing fool things like this?" I asked, less brusquely, turning his revolver over in my hand.

"Oh, let me do it! Let me do it!" he pleaded. He was still shaking there on the bench beside me.

"Then tell me *why*, first."

He tried to pull himself together slowly. His dead and passive face was more dispiriting than his hysterical and womanish tears.

"I've made a mess of everything—a terrible mess," he said, with a gulp. "It's the only way out!"

"It's a *coward's* way out!"

He drew back and looked at me, with the first vestige of personal interest.

"What do you know of me, or what I've done?" he demanded.

"I know what you were going to do! That's enough! Perhaps you're not the only man who's been up against it good and hard!"

"Talk's cheap!" The bitter finality of his tone seemed to bristle around him like a guarded embankment. But still I tried to get closer to him.

"Not so cheap as *this*!" I said, tapping the mother-of-pearl gun.

"I tell you I can't go back to it! It's no use!"

"Why not?"

"There's nothing left but—but—" He did not finish. It was broad daylight by this time. I had other things to think of.

"Look here," I said, taking in his wretchedly soiled linen, his hollowed eye-sockets, his drawn and sunken face. "What you want is a good warm bath, a hot breakfast, and then some sleep!"

His lips curled sullenly, ungratefully, as he looked at me with his dead and dispirited eyes.

"It wasn't my *stomach* brought me to this sort of thing!" he retorted.

"Life is only as deep as the viscera," I answered—but my Herbert Spencer was lost on him.

"Oh, leave me alone!" he moaned, sinking back on the bench. There was something about the youth that made still another effort worth while.

"You come and climb into a hansom with me, drive down to my hotel, and take a tub and breakfast. Then, if you can show me I'm wrong, I'll leave you alone for good and all!"

He peered at the city house-tops through the bushes, with a look of mingled horror and fear and hate. Then he drew back, like a child from a dark hallway.

"It's too late!" he groaned. "I tell you it's too late!"

"Why not try it?"

"I don't *want* to try it!" he retorted.

But I kept at him, until I had him on his feet. Even active misery was better than his earlier dead passivity. I buttoned up his coat for him, and straightened his hat on his head, as though he were a schoolboy.

"It's no use, I tell you!" he cried, in a fresh spirit of revolt. But I felt differently, as I held on to him and kept him up, and waited at the edge of the winding carriage drive for an empty hansom. The city, while we talked, had awakened into life once more. The far-off rumble grew insistent and continuous; it mounted into a roar. An early horseman or two cantered along the bridle paths. Workmen went by on the asphalted walks. A breeze stirred the leaves. The birds were singing gaily.

A passing hansom drew up at my sign, and we climbed into it. The youth lay back against the padded seat cushions, with closed eyes, with a face that seemed leaden and hopeless, burned out and dead, like ashes, as we drove briskly down through the great city, stirred and wakened into its leviathan-like life once more. It was not until Broadway roared and seethed about us that I realised just what had happened. As I had leaned back studying that burned-out youthful face I had forgotten my own fears and my own predicament. Without realising it I had made my own escape. The hansom had carried me calmly out through the gates of the park, where an ever-tightening cordon of police watched and waited.

II

The outlook was not encouraging. But I had decided to follow the thing through to a finish. So at each move and moment I kept that unhappy young man under my eye. Even when I had him safely up in a room, between four walls, I left him only for a minute or two—and that was to send quietly down to the house physician for sleeping powders.

I even looked in on my charge when he was taking his tub, and stood over him when his breakfast was sent up, and insisted that he eat at least a goodly portion of it. When he bucked on the coffee, I gave him a good nourishing silver-fizz. When he asked for another I gave it to him, and also ten grains of bromide with just half the same quantity of chloral. Then I tried to quiet him down, and fixed his pillows, and told him to forget his troubles.

But he still tossed about on the bed fretfully. Neither my assurances nor the narcotic seemed able to put his mind at rest.

Suddenly he sat up and fixed me with his unsteady and feverish eye.

"By ——, I *can't* lie here, with everything hanging over me this way!" he burst out.

I told him to keep still and go to sleep—and casually took up my morning paper and began reading it.

"I tell you I *can't* keep still until I've put this thing straight!" he persisted. I pushed him back into the bed, for I knew it was merely a matter of time before the narcotic would have him in its clutch.

"But I've got to have my say," he went on, back on the pillows. "I'm not what you think I am. I'm not a—a street loafer! My people are decent people, all of them."

I heard him add, in a meditative undertone, "Except me!"

"I know that—of course they are!" I told him, soothingly.

He was silent for a minute or two. I thought at first that he was about to fall asleep.

"What are you bothering with me for, anyway?" he suddenly broke out, as though the strangeness of what I was doing had just come home to him.

"Because I think I've been up against the same sort of thing that you've been up against," was my answer.

It left him thinking, for a few seconds of silence. It also left me thinking for an unhappy moment or two.

"I've *got* to put this thing square!" he cried again, sitting up in bed.

"Go ahead, then!" I told him resignedly, carelessly, from over my morning paper.

"My governor's quite a man in this town!" he began, inappositely. Then he broke off and laughed a bitter little laugh. "He thought he'd make *me* quite a man, too, I guess! But I wasn't built that way!"

"Who is your father?" I inquired.

"What's that to either you or me, now?" he complained with a return of peevishness.

"Then what's the use of talking at all?"

"Because you've got to see how things stand—how I'm down and out! The governor soured on me after I'd queered things in my first year at Harvard," he went on, with a sort of sullen deliberation. "Then he tried me at railroading, down on one of his little God-forsaken Mexican side-lines. Then I weakened and came back to New York, and he gave me another chance in the Wall Street office. I made a mess of things there, a horrible mess!"

"How do you mean?"

"Oh, I mean every old way! I guess I've been cursed with the governor's passion for plunging, for playing the game to the limit, without having a decent table to play it on! It's all a gamble, anyway—only they're ashamed to say so—south of Canal Street! They call it finance, or some other nice-sounding name—but they're gamblers, all of them! Take the governor. He plays his cards and juggles his pack, and shuts himself up, down there in a Wall Street office, to scheme and plot and trick, just like a 'con' man! Of course he says he has to work secretly, to safeguard his syndicate interests from the raids of the speculators, to keep his rails clear of the habitual gamblers! But that's a blind—that's just oil for his uneasy conscience—it's all graft and bunco, through and through!"

It was the same old sophistry that one may hear night and day along the Under Groove. It was the appeasing self-deceit of the man who had fallen, clutching perversely at those who still walked upright!

"I lost my grip," he went on, hopelessly, evenly. "They started calling me hard names at home. I played the races now and then, just to kill time and keep alive. My name came out in the second Penfield raid, and that made the governor worse than ever. He let loose, and said some pretty rank things—and that made me reckless! But are you listening?"

"To every word!" I answered, over my paper. Here, I mentally observed, was the second generation with a vengeance. Here was the hot-house growth of ease and opulence with its sheltering glass blown away!

"The governor dropped me, then. They all dropped me—all except Peggy!"

"Who's Peggy?" I asked.

"That's my sister," he answered, speaking more and more feverishly as he went on. "She stuck to me right through. I wanted to do the right thing by her, but—but I couldn't. She got me out of the Bucklin scrape, and paid up what I owed in the Penfield place. She knew I couldn't keep out of pool-rooms as long as I was in New York—I had to have the excitement—it was the only thing that could shake the dry rot off me! So she got me that horse ranch out in Alberta. She thought if I got out West, living that sort of life, it would help me along. I guess it would have, too. But I gave a mortgage or a note or something on the ranch before I had the title, and tried one last plunge on the Jamaica field. Luck went against me. I was in a nice mix-up. Then I got a sure-thing tip on Bob Travis's pool-room, where the Waldorf men do their betting. The mortgage people were talking ugly—I was in a horrible box. I went down to the governor's office: I pretended I wanted to see him alone. But I went when I knew he wouldn't be there. I saw my chance, and I took it. I would have been a thief, a felon, if Peggy hadn't got back what I took. I'd been drinking then—I must have been crazy. But she got the money away from me—I can't tell you how, now. It saved me from *that*, but it didn't save me from the mortgage people. So I sneaked up and let myself in, at the governor's, to tell Peggy everything. It was late at night—Peggy wasn't home from the Metropolitan. I got her pass book, and found out her bank balance. Then I dug out her cheque book, and filled in a cheque for three thousand and fifty dollars—in her handwriting. Then I signed her name to it. I took it down to Travis and told him she'd helped me out again, the same as she'd done before. Travis thought everything was all right. So he cashed the cheque!"

"And you plunged with that three thousand and fifty, and lost?"

"Yes—I lost!"

"But mightn't she still give you a chance?"

"Yes, *she* would—but the others won't."

"What others?"

"Why, Travis and the others. I haven't got to the worst of it. A 'capper' for the Gilmont stables came to me with a tip from 'Rolling Timber's' jockey that the race was cooked and his horse *had* to win. It was my last chance. I still thought I could make things right. I still had Peggy's cheque book. So I did the trick a second time, signing her name again. Travis took her paper for two thousand; every cent of it except fifty dollars went up on 'Rolling Timber.' "

He passed his lean and quivering hands down over his face feverishly.

"God, what I went through!" he groaned.

"And when the returns came in over the wire 'Rolling Timber' didn't happen to be first?"

"She *did* win!" cried the man on the bed, turning sharply round on me. "The returns had her *first*—every ticker and wire report had her first—except Travis's!"

"I don't quite follow you!"

"I'd run over to Whitehead's handbook room, to put up that extra fifty. I was going to keep *that*, to get me out of town with. But the odds of five to one were too much for me. The returns were in before I could get across the street again to Travis's. 'Rolling Timber' had won! When I got upstairs and called for my money

I saw the announcement there that 'Cedarton Sewell' had won. I told Travis he was posting false returns. He denied it. Three minutes after that the wires were humming with the corrected report. 'Cedarton Sewell's' jockey had worn a canary jacket with cherry sleeves. The jockey on 'Rolling Timber' had worn a jacket of yellow with magenta sleeves. The field report had mixed the colours, and declared 'Rolling Timber' first, instead of 'Cedarton Sewell.' I had taken my last fling . . . and I'd lost!"

Again his voice trailed away into emptiness, and the earlier gray look of hopelessness crept over his face.

"How did Travis get those field reports?" I asked.

"Same as all the other pool-rooms have to do now—over a 'phone wire and by runners," answered the man on the bed, indifferently.

"But although the tickers and handbook men announced the wrong winner, Travis was right from the first? I mean to say, he had 'Cedarton Sewell' posted for first place from the beginning?"

The man on the bed nodded his head sleepily. Then he gave vent to a short yawn.

"Why do you suppose Travis could do that?" I demanded.

"I dunno," answered the indifferent voice.

When I put down my paper and peered over at the man on the bed, his eyes were closed. He lay back on the pillow fast asleep.

III

I waited just one minute, to make sure there was no mistake about it. Then I stooped closer, and studied his face. There was nothing to fear: the man, for the time being, was dead to the world.

Then I swung round to the chair, across which he had flung his clothes. It was no time for compunctious half-measures. I lifted the garments up carefully, one by one, and as carefully went through them, pocket by pocket.

There was surprisingly little to reward my search. The youth's last penny had gone; so, apparently, had his jewelry, from scarf-pin to cuff-links.

In their place I found three folded pawn tickets. I next came upon a pool-room admission card, an oblong of pasteboard stamped "2890," and initialled "B.T.," and a slip of rough paper on which an unformed hand had written: "Play 'Rolling Timber' for first to the limit!" What he told me apparently had been the truth.

In the breast-pocket of the coat I found a scrap of paper, the paper he had held in his hand on the park bench. It was nothing more than an empty envelope. On the face of it, which had been crossed and recrossed with pencil marks, was inscribed "Percival Merrill Shaler," in a woman's handwriting. Below the name was a hurriedly pencilled number, apparently that of a district messenger office. But that was all.

I turned the envelope over in my hands, meditatively. Written across the back of the oblong of paper I made out another name, a woman's.

As I spelled out this name and thought over the memories it aroused a new colouring seemed to creep over the situation, as thoroughly as a tinted spot-light changes the character of a stage scene.

The sleeper on the bed no longer seemed a mere derelict on the streets to me. The name written on the envelope back was "Margaret Merrill Shaler."

I stooped over the sleeper, studying him as he lay there, feature by feature. There could be no mistake about it. The vague cognatic resemblance was there. I could trace it, point by point, in the heavily lined and devitalised young face, just as memory might rebuild the buoyant grace of some burned vessel from its charred and purposeless hulk. This unhappy wreck of a man I had stumbled on in Central Park was the brother of Margaret Shaler.

I looked down at the sleeper once more, as the truth of the thing filtered through my brain. There was something common and kindred, I felt, in each of us. We were each the result of a condition. The same riot of wealth, the same loose-handed pursuit of fortune, the same drunkenness for unearned increment, that had brought his type into existence, had made possible my own career and calling. He had tasted wealth without learning the meaning of restraint; he had been given leisure without the forewarning traditions of leisure; he had been cursed with a febrile energy without its appeasing outlet of labour.

My next feeling was one of vague resentment at the thought of what an impossible game the youth on the bed had been playing. He had been battering his foolish young head against one of the most craftily organised swindles in all this gigantic city of rose-wreathed and circuitous robbery. That much I knew, for there had already been an occasion when the notorious Bob Travis and I had met—and before the end of that meeting each of us had found out a little too much of the other man's moves and methods! Knowing Travis for what he was, I decided he would have nothing to gain in crushing young Shaler. Like all such gamblers, he was after money and nothing else. So if the two forged cheques were duly met Travis could be eliminated from the problem.

That left the girl herself—young Shaler's sister. She could be counted on, I felt, once she thought her brother sincere in some movement of redemption. She had, obviously, already overlooked a great deal. She had also done a great deal and what she had done had been merely to save the boy from trouble. It was safe to assume, then, that she would do even more to save him from death. And she was a girl of the right spirit: of that I had more than once had ample proof.

There was already the ghost of a chance that the two cheques had not yet been put through by Travis. The second cheque could not have been given before three o'clock in the afternoon. And that had been yesterday. Travis would stick to his pool-room while the race returns were still coming in. It was ten to one that he had stayed there until banking hours were over. In that case the first and only thing to do was to see Travis himself, get face to face with the gambler, and buy in the cheque before its repudiation at the bank turned the whole thing into an open and irretrievable offence.

I left the sleeping man locked in, with a word or two to the house detective to keep an eye on things in my room. Then I jumped into a hansom and made straight for the lair of Travis.

The more I thought of it the simpler the whole thing seemed. I even began to glow with a genial appreciation of a good deed well done. I fell to picturing the girl of the Unknown Door gazing up into my eyes, with her hand in mine, murmuring some broken phrase of gratitude. I seemed treading on air as I climbed the wide stairway that led up to the pool-room entrance.

Then earth and its realities were around me again, in the movement of a hand, in the touch of a bell-button. For as the door swung guardedly back a few inches, a burly and belligerent-eyed "thrower-out" confronted me.

"Well?" he demanded insolently, with a ragged cigar in one corner of his mouth.

"I've got to see Travis!"

"Have you?" he said, without budging.

"This is a matter of personal business," I explained.

The man grinned.

"It's pressing—important!" I persisted.

The bulldog face blinked out at me indifferently, apathetically, insolently. My patience was getting exhausted. So I pushed in farther through the half-opened door.

"Nothin' doin'!" he said, blocking my way.

"I tell you I've got to see Travis!" I repeated desperately. A look of anger took the place of insolence on the face of the czar of the under world.

"Git out o' here!" he cried, with an oath of finality.

"Not until I see Bob Travis!" I retorted.

"Git out o' this!" he bawled, bringing up a hand that looked like a ham.

I stepped back as it shot out at me. Before I could recover myself the great armoured door was slammed shut and locked in my face. I stood there, blinking at it helplessly.

It began to dawn on me that a righter of wrong, a champion of the weak and fallen, needed a cleaner record than mine if he didn't want his altruistic motives misunderstood.

IV

My first feeling of defeat, as I went slowly down the stairs and out into the street, gradually changed into one of defiance. I began to realise the absurdity of making any such dive-keeper as Travis see the disinterestedness of my position. Such things were foreign to his jackal-thoughted comprehension. He would have to be met and worsted on his own field; he would have to be fought with his own tools.

And I still had one of his tools, I told myself, as I meditatively circled the block. I still had a weapon that could make him wince, that could make the game worth while, once I had it by the handle.

The problem was to find and grasp that handle. My first clue to its whereabouts lay in the fact that Travis and his office had not fallen a victim to the false wire-report confounding "Cedarton Sewell" with "Rolling Timber." That implied a thing that I had more than once vaguely suspected. Either Travis and his associates had had a hand in the "cooking" of a race, or he was the master of some secret and subterranean system of getting race returns direct from the track. The latter seemed the more reasonable inference. The wealth of this king of pool-room keepers was indisputable; his influence was one of the accepted mysteries of the under world. Those officials of the law who had not been "greased" into servitude with his gold had been coerced into subserviency through his "politics." He had stood immune through every spasmodic fever of raid-making. He was an autocrat of his district, a buccaneer behind his bulwarks of illicit wealth.

But had the man's cunning and audacity ventured to the limit of a secret wire between his office and the track itself? That was the thing I began more and more to suspect, and that was the thing I was going to settle in my own mind once for all.

Halfway round the block I stopped and entered an office building which I felt reasonably sure abutted on the back of the Travis place. I stepped into the elevator and was let out on the top floor. There I stood before the door of a face-balm agency, in a pretence of knocking, until the elevator sank out of sight. Then I hurried to the back of the hall, where a locked door confronted me. The lock of this door I promptly picked, and found myself in a small storage-room where a narrow iron stairway led to a roof-transom. It was only the work of a minute or two before I had made my way to the roof itself.

This roof, I saw, was overshadowed by two adjoining office buildings. In other words, every move I made would be in full view of half a hundred windows. So I slipped back down the narrow iron stairway. Hanging on the wall there I had already caught sight of a pair of overalls and jacket. They were of coarse drilling, much soiled and stained, and had once been the property, I assumed, of some engineer or janitor in the building. Underneath them hung a peaked black cap, also the worse for wear. They were exactly the things I needed.

Two minutes later I emerged on the roof, roaming about with the careless self-confidence of an engineer on a casual round of inspection. In half an hour I had made my observations, looked over my ground, descended again to the storage-closet, peeled off my soiled drilling, left everything just as I found it, closed and locked the door after me, and calmly rung the bell for the elevator.

In less than four hours from the time I first stepped out of that elevator I had worked out my plan of campaign and made ready my Outfit, down to the last coil of wire. Then I bought fresh linen for young Shaler, and hurried back to the hotel with my suit-case Outfit. In the crowded rotunda, ironically enough, I brushed elbows with a bejewelled individual I knew to be a "steerer" for the Travis gambling rooms. It reminded me, as I hurried on my way upstairs, how complex and far-reaching was the machinery I was to fight against. But the thought did not disturb me. In five minutes I had shaken the drowsy youth into semi-sensibility and was plying him with a second cup of black coffee. It would have been safer, I knew, to let him sleep out his sleep. But I needed his help, little as it might be. For once I was face to face with a situation where I could not work alone.

V

I had scarcely expected a few hours of forced sleep to make a new man of young Shaler. But I had looked for a little more amiability than that of an unfed grizzly prodded out of its cave.

His first few minutes of sullen torpor gave place to a more active ugliness of temper, a sour and cynical resentment to what he kept mumbling about as my interference in his private affairs. By the time he was washed and dressed, however, the *café noir* had begun to establish its influence, and he turned and studied me with impassive distrust. There was something exasperating about his apathy, now that I was in mid-current of this new and sweeping enterprise.

"What are you trying to do, anyway?" he complained, sitting weakly down on the tumbled bed.

"I'm trying to keep you from blowing out what few brains you've got!" I retorted. He peered up at me fretfully.

"And is keeping me from doing that going to put any of this thing straight again?" he complained.

"Yes, it is," I declared. "And it's going to put *you* straight! Aren't you acting this way for a mere matter of five thousand dollars?"

"It's not the *money*!" he groaned. "It's the way I got it!"

"But suppose it's returned? Suppose you make good—to the last cent?"

"There's no supposing about it! It can't be done! Everything's gone too far!"

"It *can* be done!" I cried. "And you and I are going to do it!"

He looked at me incredulously, pityingly. "How?" he asked.

"We're going to get this money back from Travis to-day!"

"You might as well talk about getting a beefsteak back from a Bengal tiger!" He laughed a short and mirthless laugh. "What do *you* know of Travis and his ways?"

It was like arguing with a lunatic. His mind began to impress me as one that had never learned to walk by itself. He knew nothing of the primal order of things, of the Law of the Open. He sat before me there on the bed, impotent, irresponsible, exhausted, only passively conscious of the depth of his wrong-doing, one of the beautiful by-products of an age of unparalleled and arrogant wealth. But I had to stick by him now, through thick and thin.

"I know *this* about Travis and his ways," I cried, "I know that he runs a crooked game!"

The other man stared at me.

"And I also know that the five thousand dollars he got from you he got in a crooked way!"

"Who *are* you, anyway?" suddenly demanded the man on the bed.

"I'm not a coward!" was my retort. I hadn't expected enough good blood in his flaccid veins to make him wince as he did.

"But why should you want to do things like this—for me?" His life had left him wary and cynical and suspicious of his fellows.

"I'm not doing it for you!" I promptly answered him.

"For whom, then?" he asked, in wonder.

"For the woman you took this money from, for one reason!"

"Please leave that woman out of this!" he cried wrathfully.

"Why should I?"

"Because she is my sister!" I stood amazed at his perverse and foolish pride. I also resented his expression, as he looked me up and down, a little contemptuously.

"Then you have always treated her like one?" I asked. He jumped to his feet and confronted me, shaking.

"I prefer keeping her out of this, I tell you!" he raged.

"You should have preferred that two days ago!"

I saw him wilt under that unfair blow, and I almost hated myself for it.

"I won't have *her* mixed up with a beast like Travis, whatever it costs!" he doggedly declared.

"She's not our kind!" he added, after a second or two of gloomy silence. And I caught myself wondering why something within me should resent the claim that this luckless child of wealth and I stood on the same ground, and that that ground, beside the paths of Margaret Shaler, seemed as low as the Seventh Pit beside the brink of Paradise.

I looked at my comrade in crime more critically. After all, I didn't have much to work with. I even wondered if I could depend on him—if he was worth it. Then I remembered the girl who had waited for me on the inside of a barred window while I balanced over death on the end of a blackboard. I thought of the girl who had crept through an unlighted bank-corridor at my side—and my hesitation vanished.

"Look here," I said, "we're only working at cross-purposes and losing time. This gambler has got your money. He's got *more* than your money—he's got your whole family's good name and honour along with it. He got that money in a crooked game—that I know. And we both know that no moral suasion on earth or in heaven would ever make him unload. So the one thing left for us is to fight Travis with his own tools, fight fire with fire. I mean, let dog eat dog!"

"You can't touch Travis!" declared the youth. "He's below the dead-line, and he's got everything greased!"

"We *can* touch him! We can cut into him by the very knife he's cutting into other people. Listen: Travis makes a pretence of getting all his track returns by telephones and 'runners.' He protests that this sort of handbook game is all the police will let him operate. But you yourself say he has the police under his thumb. So he must have some motive for putting up that bluff. I'll tell you what that motive is: to give him an excuse for posting a late report, for announcing his returns three or four or even five minutes later than the actual wire report leaves the track!"

"But what good would that do him!"

"It does him good *because he's got a secret wire right from the race-track to the back of his own pool-room!*"

Young Shaler started up, with a little gasp.

"What's more, I have seen that wire; I've found it where it goes sneaking along a hundred feet of cornice and skulking up across a back wall and slinking down a chimney into his private office, curling and twisting out of sight like a snake trying to hide from a farmer's heel!"

"Then he gets every return from the track before his last bets are laid, before he makes his killings?"

"In nine cases out of ten he knows every winner before the last odds are flashed. Then he plays and juggles the book to suit himself. He has to drop a little, now and then, for the sheer sake of appearances. But probably you know as well as I do that he went into this thing without a thousand dollars. He now owns a quarter of a million dollars' worth of tenement houses. And that money has poured in to him, slinked and crept and skulked in to him, along one little steel wire!"

"But how could he keep it up, with that Wall Street crowd that he has?"

"Those Wall Street followers of his are plungers, blind gamblers, all of them. They have the fever of it in their blood, whether they're winning or losing. So he portions them out their bait money, like loaves to a bread line—just enough to hold them and no more. Stop for a minute to figure it out! Even a rake-up of a thousand dollars a month, for two hundred bettors, means an average of nearly seven thousand dollars a day!"

"But what on earth can we do about it?" cried the youth before me. I was beginning to infuse a little life into him after all.

"I can run a 'jumper' from that wire back behind the elevator shaft-head on the roof of the next building! I mean I can carefully adjust my instrument, equalise my current, and cut in on that wire, without Travis or his operator ever knowing it. If it were a regular Postal-Union circuit, with a quadruplex system, it wouldn't be possible; but this is a single wire. It leaves me free to 'ground it off,' to attach my relay, and to read the message there on my sounder as it comes in from the track. Two minutes later, after I've made sure of the name of the winner, written it on a slip of paper and dropped it in this pigskin cigar case down the light-well, where you'll be waiting to pick it up, I can turn back and send on the intercepted message to Travis's operator. But in the meantime you've got the name of the winner, have hurried up to the pool-room, placed your bet, and done nothing to excite the suspicion of any light-fingered gentleman in that whole gambling joint!"

Young Shaler drew in his breath sharply. He made it almost a whistle. In a moment he was on his feet, pacing the room.

"But what money have we got to bet?" he cried, with a flash of his old-time suspicion.

"I've got just eleven hundred dollars here—if we can't get a five or six-to-one shot, we'll have to hit them twice. But there'll be a ragged field to-day, with long shots enough. All we have to do is to decide on which event we intend to play!"

"And I take this eleven hundred of yours up to Travis's, and play it to the limit?" he repeated, watching me as I caught up my hat and suit-case and motioned for him to make ready.

"To the limit!" I replied, unlocking the door and seeing that the way was clear.

"But what do you get out of all this?" he still asked, in utter perplexity.

"*I get the fun of playing the game!*" was my answer. It sounded enigmatic to him, I know. It sounded enigmatic, even to my own ears, until some vague line about the shoulder and head poise of the figure in front of me brought back certain memories that my colleague of a day would never have understood.

VI

I felt almost at home again, once I had reached the roof, and began busying myself with my preparations. As I sat there in my oil-stained drill overalls, bending over the familiar old instruments, I felt that both the more dangerous and the more difficult part of my work was done.

I had taken my "line balance" and carried my No. 18 "jumper" wire to the rear of a shaft-head, where I could work more or less screened between a wall angle and a chimney row. As I sat and watched the magnetic needle of my "detecter" galvanometer dip and register the strength of the current, I tried to picture the scene that was already taking place in the pool-room below me; the crowded betting-quarters, thick with cigar smoke, the quick, mechanical calling of the odds, the posting of events, the announcing of weights and jockeys, the passing back and forth of money through the little wicketed, secretive hole in the wall, the wolfish and waiting faces, the blighted spirits gripped by the hunger of unearned gold.

As I cautiously turned back the graduated handle of my rheostat and the resistance coils were one by one thrown into circuit, I thought first of the miracle of electricity, and then of the madness that made men gamble, that made them shrink from effort and adventure, from independence of thought and action, and crawl, sick and drowsy, to the still more deadening lap of Chance. Even the life of the buccaneer, I consoled myself, was incomparably better than that of the gambler; the one was the boisterous but clarifying ripple of a busy stream; the other was the bubbling stagnation of a malodorous marsh.

Then, as I cut quietly into that little metal artery of intelligence before me, without one moment's "bleeding" of the circuit, and my Bunnell sounder started to click and clutter with the Morse reports from the far-distant race-track, I thought of the familiar scene about the level ring, the crowded grand stands bright with colour and movement, the hubbub of sound, the bookmakers and rail birds and touts and runners and gamblers, the gay-jacketed jockeys, the start, the race, the straining flanks and flying feet, the rise of the crowded benches and the roar of voices at the finish.

Then I gave all my attention once more to the spasmodic "send" of the track operator on the far end of the wire, making careful note of his characteristic tricks and slurs, for the "event" on which we had banked everything was at hand. This man's "send," I realised, would have to be imitated to a nicety as I sat there forwarding my intercepted message—for to the trained ear the sound of a Morse key is as variable and as characteristic as the modulations of a human voice.

But when the moment came, my hand was as steady as though I had been pounding the brass with the opening paragraph of a consular report. I sent the arrested dots and dashes hurrying on their way again, and when the first lull came I cut out my "jumper," patched together the breach I had made in the circuit, flung my tools into the suit-case, and hurried back across the roof to the transom door, elated with a sense of victory.

As I opened that narrow door, I came to a sudden standstill, and the elation went out of my body. For there, half-way up the stairway, stood a burly giant of an engineer, in blue jeans. He advanced another step or two with his arms akimbo, gazing at me with a look of silent rage and resentment. He made me a bit uneasy.

"Come right in!" he called out mockingly. I realised, as I looked down at him, that he was a veritable Hercules in strength.

"And were yuh lookin' for me?" he demanded, with a beguiling coyness that warned me he was only holding back for some final spring.

"I'm looking for anybody who'll give me a hand up with this wire coil!" I equivocated, with a pretence of ignoring his wrath.

"Then how did you get that door open?" he suddenly demanded. He was a hare-brained autocrat, I saw, merely jealous of his domain and his authority.

"What do I know about your door?" I bawled back at him. It began to madden me to think the fool was making me lose valuable time. But he was obdurate.

"You opened that door!" he howled menacingly.

"I've got bigger jobs than smashing in doors and talking to fools! Do you think I'm a house-breaker?"

"What are yuh, then?"

"I'm a Postal-Union lineman, you idiot—and I've got a wire to string across to the Biddle Building!"

"Then where's your permit?"

He came up the narrow iron stairs, slowly, suspiciously.

"Are you going to give me a hand with that wire coil?" I demanded impatiently, without so much as a further look at him.

"Open that suit-case!" he commanded.

Here was a new and unexpected peril. If my enemy possessed a technical knowledge of electrical appliances he would see at a glance that my Outfit was something more than a lineman's tools.

But there was no getting away from him. It resolved itself into the sheer and final chance of whether or not the man could spot a wire-tapper's outfit when he saw one.

"Open that case!" he repeated.

I did as he ordered, petulantly, but with no show of resistance. Yet for a moment or two my heart was in my mouth. He seemed less sceptical as he looked down at the instruments. I began to breathe again.

"Now where's this wire coil yuh're talkin' of?"

"Hanging over that wall there!" And I pointed to the south side of the roof where a power wire swayed loose on its insulator. The giant got slowly down on his hands and knees and peered along the roof ledge in search of it. My chance had come.

I was through the transom door before he had time to look up. I had the hasp snapped shut over the great iron staple and was peeling off my suit of drilling before he got to the stair head. I could hear his thunderous kicks and blows on the door above me as I caught up my hat and coat and suit-case. I could hear his bellow and oath of rage as I locked the storage-closet door behind me, went to the elevator, and rang the bell. I descended to the ground floor, whistling, passing out to the street as decorously as a travelling salesman leaving a jobber's office.

VII

For the second time that day, however, my elation was short-lived. My heart sank as I stepped up to the four-wheeler that had been left waiting for us on the far side of the block. Shaler was not there. He was not in the carriage; he was nowhere in sight. He had failed me in some last moment of emergency!

As I stood there, in helpless bewilderment, an officer in uniform plucked me by the sleeve. The sight of him made my blood run cold. For a brief moment, before he started on his patrol down the square once more, the faintest shadow of a smile played about his pugnacious Celtic mouth.

"Your friend's in Nicchia's *café*!" he had said knowingly, and yet casually, as he touched my arm and passed on.

It took me a minute or two to understand just what he meant.

154

Then I turned westward for one block, rounded the corner, and entered Nicchia's by a side door. Shaler was there, waiting for me, in a little room behind the telephone-booth. There was something fiercely exultant in his white young face.

"Quick, or it'll be too late!" he cried, leading me down through a billiard-room to a narrow corridor.

"Hurry, man, hurry! They're after us!" he whispered, and he ran through the corridor and mounted a flight of steps.

"Who?" I asked, as I raced after him. He was no longer the listless being of three hours before.

"Travis—all of them!" he cried, as he led the way into a many-odoured kitchen where two Italian cooks repeated orders from a stream of hurrying waiters.

"But why? Why?" I demanded, as I followed him through a door out into a back alley and then through another door and a corridor into the street itself. He did not stop to answer.

"You made your bet? You got your money up?" I still persisted, as he motioned for a passing hansom.

"The money went up on a twelve-to-one-shot," he exulted, as I climbed into the cab after him, breathless. We swung about, at an order from Shaler, and tore toward the Grand Central Station. "We stuck him—to the hilt!" he repeated, with a little gasp of indignation tempered with triumph.

"Then why—then what's all this fuss for?" I demanded. I glanced down and noticed for the first time that young Shaler's right hand was bound up in a handkerchief.

"It's because I can't stay in this town for half an hour!" he cried. "He's setting every thug and floater of his, north of Canal Street, after me! They're holding him down there—he's going on like a wild man!"

"But what happened?"

"He's after my scalp—he says he'll get me where I belong! But I'll fool him!"

There was indeed a metamorphosis!

"What happened?—tell me what happened!" I repeated, in a cross between bewilderment and exasperation.

For answer, he flung three one-hundred-dollar bills into my lap. I caught them up and looked at them, as I listened to the man at my side.

"Everything went just as you said it would. I got Dorlon, the cashier, to the wicket when I put up my money. He told me my two cheques had never been put through. Then my thirteen-thousand-dollar *coup* against his book hit him so hard he agreed to sell the cheques back at face value. He had to keep enough in the bank, he said, until Travis came in and fattened it up again. So he passed through the two cheques. He was counting out the money to me, bill by bill, when Travis shot in from downstairs. I'd got the two cheques and the three one-hundred-dollar bills in my hand. Travis fought to get them back—he intended to bleed my folks with the bad paper—he knew it was all wrong, from the first!"

He stopped for breath. "Go on!" I cried.

"I got away with what I held, and fought for it. I tore the cheques up, under his nose. Then he called me a forger and a lot of other stuff. Then I lost my head and let loose on him and told him *to get that track-wire out of his chimney!*"

I sat up with a whistle.

"That set him raving—it was hitting him where he lived. He jumped for me like a hyena. I hit him—just once. He tried to draw a revolver when he was down. But the crowd jumped in on him, smothered him. They couldn't make out what the row was. Neither could his bouncers. They threw me out before Travis could get free again. A policeman who stood in with Travis picked me up and helped me into Nicchia's. He advised me to cool down, and kept telling me not to be a fool and make a charge. Then he tipped me off how to get through the back way!"

"And where are you going now?"

He looked at me in wonder.

"I'm going to get just as far away from New York as I can get! I've had my chance, and won! I've won, but it has cost me something! I know what Travis is, and I know what he'd like to do! But I'll fool him, or know the reason why!"

"Then where are you going?"

"I'm going to take the Transcontinental Express from Montreal, to-morrow, for Calgary. And when I get to Calgary I'm going to team forty-five miles overland to that horse ranch of mine!"

A silence fell over him, and, as we swung round into Forty-second Street I put the three bills back in his hand. He held them, mechanically, unconsciously, his thoughts elsewhere.

"You'll need this," I explained. But still he did not look at them.

"I want you to go up and explain to her—to Peggy," he said in a lowered and more deliberate tone. Then he looked down at the bills, and the faintest touch of colour came into his lean cheek.

"It'll take me a good long time, I guess, to square this with you, to pay all these things back! But I'll do it, if you give me time! I'll do it—or my name isn't Shaler."

We looked at each other for a moment or two. Then we shook hands, man to man.

"I've been a fool," he broke out bitterly. "All kinds of a fool—but I want you to tell her everything, as well as you can!"

A moment later the great, vaulted station had swallowed him up, and I sat back in the hansom, alone, thinking of the girl of the Unknown Door, softly dreaming of the mission thrust upon me, yet half-dreading the meeting that already seemed to make life over for me.

CHAPTER EIGHT
THE ADVENTURE OF THE END AND THE BEGINNING

I

Good old Dinney, dog-like, faithful old Dinney, had burrowed his way up into New York under the very noses of the Central Office men. He had come without sign or warning. So I'd taken the next day off, to lead him about like the Hoosier he was, to show him the wonders of the Under Groove. I wanted to see his eyes pop at the free-and-easy way things were done in the East. And they did.

It so fell out at the end of our day that we had drifted into a Third Avenue "all-night" drug-store for one last glimpse of life in the raw.

I sat drowsily back against the greasy woodwork of the telephone-booth, close beside my old-time "finder" and "stick-up," watching the scene; for an all-night drug-store, where life uncovers itself bare to the buff, is never a stage to be despised.

It held me spellbound, just as a boiling volcano crater might. In it, hour by hour, kept bubbling up an under world that is seldom elsewhere revealed to man. Through it crowded and limped and thronged the submerged spirits of earth, crying for the only joy they knew of—the gloomy joy that comes out of glass bottles, and can be bought with money.

First came "Dopey" Binner, the dummy-chucker and acid-man, side by side with "Spider" Grout, the professional fit-thrower. As they lined up at the tarnished "fountain" for their frugal cup of chocolate (lavishly thickened with fuller's earth) they were followed by a mulatto cocaine-snuffer, mumbling for a dime's worth of "Tennessee." Then two "stuss-game" players perched their ragged hulks on the worn and greasy counter-stools and demanded French brandy and arsenic. Then a drunken "schlaum-worker" maundered in and asked for bromo-seltzer. But he had to wait there, wagging his nerveless head, until one "Shorty" Harris, the second-story man, made the incongruous purchase of a package of bird-seed. And while Whispering Woodsey, the ex-yegg, was buying a two-ounce bottle of creosote for "jigging" purposes, a blue-lipped and dishevelled street-woman with yellow hair that

158

showed almost purplish-black at the roots staggered in and gasped for aromatic spirits of ammonia. Then a long-nosed, furtive-eyed Russian Jew "blotta" drifted in from the Bowery, showing his teeth like a weasel, and making it known that he was after chloral-hydrate drops. Dinney, eyeing him with a grunt of disdain, ventured the belief that he was a beauty to be in the "knock-out" business.

Through the ever-busy door next came a Bowery hall-barker, fretting for the opium trochees that brought him nightly rest. Then came a trained nurse in uniform, crisp, impersonal, intent on her own duties and her own thoughts, to hurry away again with a packet of antipyrine tablets. In the doorway she brushed by two sullen-faced "slough-beaters," who promptly made way for her, for to the Under Groove the uniform invariably spells awe.

Then came a leaden-faced, staring-eyed insomniac after his favourite narcotic, and a ragged "lemon-steerer" for his little wooden box of low-grade opium-pills—all creeping in from the main current of the open street and squatting on the row of wooden counter-stools, and then drifting out again into the quiet and darkness of the night. And we kept watching them as they sat on that row of stools as placid-eyed as a rookery of Polovina seals. There they came and went, there they drowsed and swayed and stirred and drowsed again, as the content that came out of carboys and the joy that could be poured from bottles crept through their flaccid veins—chloral-drinkers and pill-eaters, needle-pumpers and cocaine-snuffers, neurotics and inebriates, Under Groove mendicants and adventurers. Scarcely a ripple stirred the line as a purple-faced hulk of a man half-fell, half-staggered in through the street door and panted and wheezed for strychnine. They watched him for a moment as he gulped down the stimulant that lashed and stirred his overdriven heart back to life. For one moment they blinked at him with their dead and indifferent eyes. Then they lapsed back into their world of money-bought dreams, or went shuffling moodily out and down to their under world once more.

Then another figure entered, one in some way different from the others. He was a small man, with rounded shoulders and a thin, hooked nose. His face was as colourless as ashes, and slightly pitted with smallpox. He stopped just inside the door, and studied the place for a moment or two. Then he sidled up to the slow-eyed, gross-necked, shining-pated German "doctor" who stood behind the counter taking his dues and dispensing his wares, as impassive as Fate itself. It was then that I noticed the newcomer's clothes were stained and eaten with acid-burns.

So low and guttural was the newcomer's voice, for so small a body, that both Dinney and I turned to stare at him. Then, as he gave his order, all our interest in his voice died away. We were listening suddenly, not to how he spoke, but to *what* he spoke, marking each word and syllable he was uttering.

For he was quietly and deliberately buying over the counter before us five ounces of pure glycerin, ten ounces of nitric acid, and fourteen ounces of sulphuric.

Dinney's eye met mine for the fraction of a second. Then we watched the man as he gathered his bottles and distributed them in the different pockets of his overcoat. For Dinney knew as well as I did that those three ingredients, properly blended, made a preparation in which we ourselves had once been more or less intimately interested. When combined in due proportion they were known as nitric ether. They were the $C_3H_5O_3(NO_2)_3$ of the chemist, the "oil" or "soup" of the gentlemen of the Under Groove, the nitro-glycerin of the world at large.

So, with one impulse, Dinney and I started up, stretched our bodies in a feint at drowsiness, and then casually sauntered out into the night on the heels of the man with the pitted face. We had each inwardly decided, without a word to the other, that the man in front of us was a personage worthy of being kept in sight.

II

We shadowed the man eastward, block by block. I could hear Dinney chuckling in his throat every now and then, as happy as a house-dog out for a run. Then our quarry turned south for a block, and again swung eastward, through a low and squalid side street of shuttered shop-fronts and neglected gas-lamps. But still we followed him, keeping well back, out of sight.

We rounded a corner just in time to behold him disappear into a basement area that seemed as narrow and dark as a well. There our pursuit had to end. But twenty minutes later he reappeared, passing within six feet of us as he circled the corner where we stood. Dinney was for going after him then and there, but I called him back. Dinney meant well, but his ways were rough and ready. His methods were apt to be rudimentary, and his thinking was usually done after the event, when thought is sometimes painful. So I took him in hand and explained to him how there might be more to learn from our new friend's basement den than from his open-air and above-ground movements. When you know a man's "fence" you know the man.

Yet down a steep little flight of steps we saw nothing more than a cellar cobbler shop. I decided, none the less, that it might be worth while to look a little farther into this cobbler shop. So I left Dinney posted on guard, and set to work.

In two minutes I had the heavy, old-fashioned iron lock opened, and no damage done. Once inside I shut the door and restored the lock bar. Then sure of not being disturbed, I played my pocket light about the place. The first room, with its cobbler's bench and smooth-worn stool and window full of old shoes, was innocent-looking enough.

Behind this room, however, was a second one. This, I soon saw, was of a somewhat different character. For here I stumbled upon an antique-looking hand-press, a font or two of type, and a few bales of paper. A vague odour of benzine greeted my nostrils. Under a shelf piled up with pamphlets and small "dodgers" were a couch and a dirty blanket. Near by were an oil stove and a cupboard of coarse dishes. On the press itself stood an ink-stained proof, with the heading: "CHTO IZ TOVO." What it meant I could not tell. I took it to be some sort of Russian revolutionary tract, in course of production.

This belief was verified by a cursory glance over the shelf. The little den was a hotbed of anarchistic literature, a well-spring of inspiration, obviously, for some band of "Reds" who had seeped in over Ellis Island, and were waiting for their day of reckoning. I took down one of the pamphlets, haphazard, and glanced through it. A sheet or two of paper fell to the floor as I riffled the pages through my fingers.

I stooped and picked them up. One was a letter from the New York *Times*, containing the printed complaint of a number of Russians against being arrested for selling "Rusky Golos" on the city streets. The other slips were copies of a carefully and laboriously penned letter, as mechanically executed as the lines of a schoolgirl's writing-book. They were written as a foreign hand might write English, or as a dull-witted boy might copy a text which he had not altogether comprehended.

But once I had run my eye over the opening sentences before me I no longer wasted time on the mere handwriting. It was the context itself that held me spellbound.

"Read this letter without moving. I am a desperate man taking a last chance. The valise in my hands holds 48 ounces of nitro-glycerin and 12 fulminate caps. When I drop it an explosion will at once take place. It will wreck the building and kill both of us. I am going blind, and must have money to finish my work. Turn back to your vault, without speaking, and put six thousand dollars on the end of your desk nearest me. If you do this, without calling out, or trying to escape or give an alarm, no harm will come to you. If you follow me before I am out of the building you will be blown to Eternity. You got this money without working for it. It's as much mine as yours. If you argue, or touch a bell, the valise will fall. If you shoot it will be the same. I want nothing but the money. Act quick, or this sentence is the last you will ever read on earth!"

* * * *

There were three copies of the inscription, each a duplicate of the others. I replaced them between the pages of the pamphlet, and put the pamphlet back on the shelf, with a laugh over the naïve mind which entered into such an inopportune argument on capitalism and yet forbade any continuance of a too one-sided debate. Then I turned quickly to the door in the rear wooden partition and entered the third room of what seemed a series of underground dens.

This third room was small and foul-smelling, yet everything about it appeared incongruously clean and orderly. Like the second room, too, it was equipped with electric lighting. Through all its mingled odours ran one acrid and significant overtone of smell. It suggested to me, even before my eyes had peered about the place, some hint of the necessity for the electrics and the cleanness.

I was in an underground laboratory of high explosives, a den of fulminates, a veritable arsenal of the most dangerous compounds known to man.

Down the centre of the room ran a wide wooden table, partly covered with a rubber sheet. On the ends of this table, beyond the rubber, stood retorts and canisters, a couple of filters, a case of test tubes, a pestle and mortar, an assortment of labelled bottles, a wooden paddle, a book of litmus paper, a mixing bowl or two. To the right of the table was a tap and sink, to the left a row of shelves holding half a dozen tin boxes, all carefully numbered, and four demijohns encased in wood. Beside them I found a number of electric detonators, made of copper wire attached to a hard plug of sulphur and ground glass, holding a fragment of platinum wire, for a resistance point. Beside these, again, stood a chess-box full of giant-caps, a tin of empty copper capsules, a fuse-crimper, and a bundle or two of what looked like cotton fibre. I ventured to feel this fibre with gentle and cautious fingers. I found it hard to the touch, considerably less flexible than ordinary cotton. I also noticed, as I guardedly rubbed a strand of it in the dark, that it grew slightly luminous under friction.

This left no shadow of doubt in my mind. The stuff before me was gun-cotton. I was face to face with some of the most violent and treacherous fulminates known to science. I was in a dungeon of undelimited dangers. One jar of a chair, one scrape of a boot-heel, might spell disaster.

It was with the utmost caution that I moved about that cave of perils. On a piece of old woollen blanket rested a rubber bag with a vulcanised screw-top. In front of me lay a blue bottle, carefully swathed in flannel. I knew little enough about explosives, but I knew that nitrogen iodide was a mixture so sensitive that it detonated, with terrible force, when brushed with even the end of a feather. I knew that common potassium carbonate, stirred into a boiling solution of picric acid in water, yielded crystals of potassium picrate, one of the most sensitive explosive compounds made. I was sophisticated enough to realise that the box of cleaned wheat-bran on the table beside me was for some future mixing with chlorate of potash, together with a sprinkling of potassium nitrate. It would result in one of the most unstable, the most dangerous, of all fulminating engines of destruction.

I was still bending over the table when a sudden, sharp sound, like the rattle of gravel against the shop-front window, warned me of approaching danger. The novelty of my discoveries had made me forget the hurrying minutes. I had overstayed my time. It might be the pitted-faced man returning. He was coming to corner me even before I could get to the open, away from that den of dangers.

I first snapped out my light. Then I caught up my Colt and held it ready. Then I edged my way cautiously but quickly to the door. I got through it safely, and closed it behind me. I was just groping my way about the remoter side of the printing-press, breathing more freely and concluding it was merely Dinney giving me a timely warning, when a key grated in the lock of the street door, and it was opened and closed again.

I could hear the advancing steps as I crouched back behind the press, with my Colt held ready, straight before me. There was no place to hide; there was no immediate way of escape. The turn of a hand might bring us face to face in the white light of the electrics. And the owner of that underground arsenal was a gentleman I had little desire to meet at such a moment. So I waited, scarcely daring to breathe.

I could have reached out my hand and touched him, he passed so close to me as he crossed the press-room, feeling his way along the wall. He was breathing heavily, as though he had been running. I could hear an inarticulate mumble from his lips as he opened the laboratory door and shut it after him.

The moment was mine, and I made the most of it. I darted quickly but noiselessly to the cobbler's room, and unbolted the street door, which he had locked behind him. Then I slipped out, equally as noiselessly, and up the steps to the sidewalk.

There I found Dinney in a blue funk, on the verge of coming after me.

"Get under cover somewhere," he whispered. "There's somebody else stalkin' this fence!"

"What makes you say that?" was my question, as I led him into the shadow of a shuttered shop-front overhung by a tattered canvas awning.

"It may be a plain-clothes man—this ain't my huntin' ground—*but somebody passed that shop three times!*"

I left Dinney under the awning and worked my way nearer the basement again. I couldn't help thinking, as I backed into the shadow of a court-alley doorway, of those over-fed carriage folk who whined that there was nothing gripping and picturesque and dramatic left in life. I couldn't help remembering, as I waited there, what half an hour in an all-night drug-store had brought me up against. For as I watched that grimy little basement front, as dark as a well, I felt that strange happenings had centred about it, and that still stranger things were going to bubble up out of its black depths.

III

I had not long to wait. As I stood there, hidden from sight, I saw the man with the pitted face mount to the street, peer cautiously east and west, and then descend to his burrow again. I passed Dinney the sign, and waited for the next move from the basement stairs.

The second time our quarry came up he carried in his right hand a small carpet-bag. I drew back deeper into the doorway until he passed.

As I waited there, with my body pressed flat against the panels, making ready to start after him, an unusual thing happened. The door behind me opened, slowly and silently. I could feel it give way on its hinges, inch by inch, and the sudden little draught of air that swept through the court alley.

A sense of vague yet undefined danger flashed through me with the quickness of light. It was far from a pleasant feeling, yet I debated, for a second or two, just what move to make. At the same moment a huge hand reached out and clutched at the shoulder of my coat. Almost involuntarily my body ducked and wheeled, for there was something electrifying, revolting, gorgonian, in that soundless hand-clutch. It left me tense and tingling with terror.

At the precise moment that I so apprehensively ducked and wheeled about there crushed down through the stiff felt of my hat what must have been the end of a black-jack. I had ducked in the nick of time. The blow had fallen short. Yet I caught sight of a looming figure in the doorway in front of me. Before it could strike again I had my Colt out and was once more square on my feet. But the door slammed shut in my face, quick as thought. I could hear the angry mutter of an oath and the slide of a bolt.

The sound of that brief encounter brought Dinney to my side on the double quick, but I held him back. We had other fish to fry. We had no time for side issues. This, after all, was a triviality to be looked into later.

By the time we recovered our senses and went scurrying down the street after the man with the carpet-bag, a precious minute had come and gone. He was already out of sight. The interval had been brief, but in that interval the fugitive had escaped us. We had crowed too soon. We had already lost our trail.

We circled and sniffed and doubled about the block like a pair of restive beagles on a stale scent. We drifted and waited and searched about the neighbourhood for an hour. But nothing came of it. No one appeared. Nothing out of the usual occurred. And we suddenly woke up to the fact that we were tired and sleepy. So we did the only natural thing left for us to do. We went home and went to bed.

It was in the morning papers that I read how one Emil Goldberg, a Third Avenue pawnbroker and diamond merchant, had been held up, that night, while working late over his books. A stranger had entered his shop, carrying a small carpet-bag. He had then handed Goldberg a letter, demanding money, and threatening that the bag, which was filled with dynamite and giant-caps, would be dropped if an alarm was raised.

The pawnbroker had saved the bulk of his fortune by declaring the time-lock already set on his safe for the night. But the thief had carried away three hundred dollars in bills. This much Goldberg had surrendered for the sake of his family, sleeping directly over the man with the bag of dynamite. There was no clue to the robber, no clue, that is, beyond the letter he had handed to the pawnbroker. This letter the morning papers reproduced.

It was a verbatim copy of the one I had read in the little basement beside the old printing-press.

"And to think we missed all that!" said Dinney, regretfully stroking his honest and obtuse old chin, when I took the report in to him and read it from the foot of the bed.

"*That* was only the overture, Dinney, my boy!" I told him. "And we're going to be in on the main act, or we're not worth our salt!"

IV

Two hours later I was back in the neighbourhood of that East Side cobbler's basement—"like a farm dog with a day off, round his favourite ground-hog hole," as Dinney put it, "and dyin' for something to bark at!"

A thick and heavy water-front fog, drifting up from the East River, had for once cleared the street of its shawled figures lounging about tenement doorways and its customary groups of saloon-corner loafers. We could pace the dingy blocks unobserved and unmolested, shut in by the heavy pall that left the city in a sort of phantasmal quietness.

So more than once we were able to direct a casual yet critical glance down the cobbler's steep little stairs. And there on his stool, as we looked, sat the man with the pitted face, hard at work with his hammer and awl, pounding pegs into a shoe-heel. So quietly and contentedly did he labour, so satisfied did he appear to be with that sedentary occupation, that the things of the night before, for one fleeting moment, seemed hard to believe. But a second and more leisurely view of him left no chance for a mistake. The man at work on the cobbler's stool was the man I had followed out of the all-night drug-store—the man who had passed out of sight with the carpet-bag.

Yet no new avenue of advance opened up before us. Only once, during all the morning, did we see any one enter his shop. This visitor was a thin and quick-moving little man, so small as to seem almost a dwarf. His pinched and angular face was shaved clean—the most noticeable thing about it was its pallor. Over his arm he had carried a black overcoat. When he reappeared, twenty minutes later, I noticed the overcoat had been left behind. My first impulse, as he passed out of sight round the corner, was to follow him. But on second thought I decided it would be fruitless, through such a fog and in such a quarter of the city.

I knew, half an hour later, that my decision had not been a mistake. For at the end of that time the pitted-faced man himself appeared up the steps. In his right hand he carried a black leather valise. His left hand was in his pocket—the pocket of the black overcoat his morning's visitor had carried in to him. This new garment seemed to convert him into a man of the world. At one stroke it seemed to make him a person of respectability, covering his ill-fitting and acid-stained clothes and converting him into one of the mediocre-clad mediocrities of our crowded city life.

I watched the thin and sombre figure stride to the corner, turn, and start southward through the yellow vapour, like a man with a fixed and clearly defined purpose. Dinney, at a hint from me,

167

crossed the street, and drifted aimlessly onward, almost opposite him. Before we had gone two blocks I could make out a second figure following after Dinney, not a hundred yards behind him.

There crept through me the feeling that something vague but vast was impending. Yet the memory of that fourth figure worried me. There was something unsettling in the thought of this secondary mystery. The sheer convolutions of such espionage puzzled and bewildered me.

When the man with the black bag turned westward, and Dinney, on the opposite side of the street, did likewise, I saw the unknown fourth figure was doing the same.

I pulled my hat low over my eyes and quickened my pace when once sure of this. Then I crossed toward Dinney at an angle, so that my path and that of the interloper must eventually impinge. I caught a sideview of the stalwart-shouldered giant in a black derby and a double-breasted sack coat, as we loomed together like two fog-bound liners. Then I veered and fell back. For in the stalking giant I saw and recognised my adversary of the Winnett *coup*. It was Miron, my old-time enemy, the smoothest come-on man in all New York.

A second sense of plotting and counter-plotting took possession of me. Three men were passing through the fog-bound streets of lower New York, each on his own secret mission, each oblivious of the other. It was the stalker twice stalked; it was a procession to make the gods laugh.

But at a breath everything seemed to change. All thought of humour suddenly withered out of the situation. All chance for leisurely psychologising over the tableau became a thing of the past.

The man with the black valise had crossed the street and turned abruptly and unexpectedly in between two great granite pillars. Those two pillars stood, I saw, beside the entrance to the Traders' Standard Trust Company.

There was no time for action, for interference, for raising an alarm. The man was swallowed up by the great bank building before I realised the meaning of it all. I saw Dinney walk on for about fifty feet, and then slowly wheel about and retrace his steps. He passed Miron face to face, without suspecting, without comprehending. His eye was fixed on a figure standing close beside one of the granite

168

pillars. It was the figure of the little white-faced man who had left the overcoat in the cobbler's shop.

Through the fog, half-way down the block, I made out a patrolman on his beat. Dinney also saw him, and again turned leisurely about, passing in front of the bank. I would have thrown him a sign, or even called out to him, but there was no time for it.

I had started across the street, when the man with the black bag dodged out between the bank doors. He had not been inside the place for more than six minutes—seven or eight, at the outside. But as he darted out between the doors he dropped a packet into the black valise and snapped it shut. Then he swung about the pillar sharply, and as he did so he brushed against the little white-faced man waiting there. Not a sign or word passed between them. But as the pitted-faced man ran eastward he had nothing in his hands. The other man sauntered westward with a black bag.

The movement was followed by one of those brief but ominous breathing-spaces of silence which precede the ordained and implacable explosion, by one of those lulls which come before the first blast of the storm. Then suddenly the bank doors seemed to volley hatless and excited men into the street. They saw the running figure and made after it. The bark of a pistol sounded out above their angry cries. An alarm-gong cluttered and clanged and throbbed. The patrolman saw the rout and joined it. The pitted-faced man raced on, with the crowd at his heels, like a pack of hounds.

But it was not this that held me rooted to the spot. What held me spellbound was the quick and decisive move of Dinney, as he descended on the unmolested man with the black bag. As he gripped the valise by the handle, and tore it from the other's grasp with his right hand, his left swung in a foreshortening semicircle, fair against the white-skinned head. The little man crumpled down on his knees and fell slowly forward, flat on the sidewalk.

Where Miron loomed from I never knew. The shifts of that kaleidoscopic scene had been so rapid that I could not follow each movement. But I saw and knew that Miron and Dinney were together, that they had closed in on one another in a sudden, unlooked-for second encounter. Before I realised the full meaning of this I heard the crack of a revolver shot. Then I saw Miron catch at the black bag. It seemed to come away at his angry jerk without resistance. Before I could quite understand that the struggle was over I saw him wheel about and pass quickly in through the door of a huge warehouse, flinging his gun out to the street-gutter as he went.

It wasn't until the door had closed on him that I made out the figure of Dinney, poor, old, faithful, dog-like Dinney, fallen across the curbstones, red and stained with his own blood.

Had he been dying and calling for help I don't think I could have waited. But one idea dominated my body and mind, but one primitive passion swayed me; that was to find and meet the enemy who had struck down one of my kind, to strike back the blow that had fallen on a comrade. My one desire, stronger than the love of life itself, was to meet this man Miron and have it out with him to the bitter end.

I sprang in through the doors. The elevator was high in the shaft. So I swung about and mounted the stairs, two steps at a time. An "overhead guerilla" like Miron, I intuitively felt, would make for the roof. In that case he had gone to the top story by elevator and was already making his escape to the open somewhere up among the water-tanks and roof-walls. The thought maddened me. I saw the elevator go down, empty. A youth on a box, squatting over a paper novel, was all it held. He knew nothing, suspected nothing. I began to wonder, vaguely, as I mounted higher and higher and the breath left my body, if other eyes on the street below had seen that assault and counter-assault. But I scarcely cared. All I wanted now was Miron, and I wanted him before the law had found him out or its officers crowded up and came between us.

I was not wrong about the roof. I found the door to a top-story wash-room had been forced open, and the screws torn away from one end of an iron bar across the window. This window was five feet higher than the adjoining roof. Miron was there, somewhere along that lonely skyline. He was there, not more than two minutes before me—perhaps not even that.

I had my breath again, and my grip on actualities, by the time I clambered out through the window-bars and dropped to the roof. Everything had come about so quickly, with such bewildering changes, that I had scarcely realised the full meaning of things. The thick fog, the quietness of the streets, the mysteriousness of our mission, had draped each scene in unreality. A feeling, as of walking through nightmare, a sense of being a ghost in a fog-bound

170

world of ghosts, had crept over me. But now all existence narrowed down to one path, and that path led to the giant-like man hiding somewhere on the roofs before me, skulking about under the open sky like a cornered wharf rat, waiting, perhaps, for just some such meeting as I was at last crowding upon him.

V

I noticed, for the first time, that the fog had given way to a cold and steady rain. It pattered heavy and mournful on the tin roof about me. The low clouds, marching from east to west, deepened the gloom of the late afternoon. I felt isolated, alone, as though I had left the world far behind me. That broken line of roofs under the pouring heavens seemed as desolate as a glacial moraine.

A moment's study showed me that Miron could have advanced in only one direction. That was straight westward over six roofs along the less broken skyline. Beyond the sixth roof rose a blank wall, thirty feet upward. Somewhere amid the water-tanks and chimney-tops and coping-tiles and shaft-heads between that blank wall and me my enemy was to be found.

I seemed to foreknow that the two of us were to meet there. Something forewarned me that the blotted ledger of Destiny was going to be balanced there, alone in the pouring rain. I did not shrink back from it. I wasn't afraid of it. I gloried in it, almost, as something Promethean, as something above the sordid thieveries of the street that had tainted and demeaned so many years of life, as something that might end the enigma of my erratic and unrelated existence.

I crept forward through the beating rain, cautiously, from barrier to barrier, half-ready for any surprise. As the area between me and the blank wall grew narrower and narrower I felt assured I must be advancing nearer and nearer my opponent. I even began to speculate on what his method of defence would be: on how he would meet me, on what we might say to each other, before the end. Then I wondered how long we would be left free there, before interference, before the sleepy-eyed elevator boy suspected and raised an alarm, before the police and the people from the street followed up this second trail and shut us in.

Then I drew back, of a sudden, with a little gasp of wonder. For there, above the coping wall in front of me, making no effort toward concealment, appeared the colossal figure of Miron. From one hand swung the black valise; from the other trailed two heavy-gauge electric wires covered with insulation rubber. They were twisted together into one coil, and had been cut away, obviously, from somewhere along the roof.

He walked steadily along the coping-stones until he came to the back wall. He stood there, looking down, the rain dripping from his black hat-rim, his clothes sodden and heavy with water.

I could see, as I whipped out my Colt, just what his plan was. He meant to fasten his wire coil to the roof and lower himself over the edge, to the foot of the blank wall below.

I was within ten feet of him, and had my drop on him, before he slowly turned and looked at me. He stood there, outlined against the gray sky, huge, titanic, sullen. He gazed at my pointing revolver without so much as a wince.

"Come down!" I commanded, advancing still closer as I spoke. I commanded myself to keep calm and self-contained. But my voice shook, foolishly, weakly, with its pent-up feeling.

"Keep away from me!" he warned, with a wave of his huge hand.

"Come down!" I repeated, "and come quick!"

I could feel some inner white rage of hatred creeping through my very bones. One twitch of a forefinger and the thing was done. I wondered how long I could hold out.

He still looked at me, without fright, apparently without comprehension of his danger. He still stood there silhouetted against the gray light, the rain dripping from his coat and hat-rim, his face colourless, his eyes slow and sullenly defiant.

"You're a fool!" he cried, unperturbed by my advancing revolver barrel. Something about his poise made me suddenly wonder if he had a confederate at hand, if he held some new card up his sleeve. It was time, I felt, to settle the whole business, once for all.

He held the black valise up before him grimly.

"D'you know what's in this?" he asked.

"Come down!" I repeated.

"There's enough pure soup in here to blow this whole d——d building into eternity!"

He looked down at me without moving.

"And you and me with it!" he added, lifting the valise up until it swayed on a level with his waist line.

"And one stir from you and I'll drop it! I don't care what it costs! D'you understand? One stir!"

His challenge threw me back like a blow in the face. Up to that moment I had scarcely given a thought to the black bag and what it held—I had scarcely given a thought to anything. My one obsession had been to find and confront him, to have it out with him and over for all time.

It was not fear that crept through me; it was merely a more comprehensive weighing of chances, a more deliberate realisation of what I had to face. I had long since learned that the trails of the under world were tragic trails. They led always to one end. They led through a jungle of feral life where one greed preyed on another, where sooner or later the weak went down before the strong. Yet mockingly, through it all, the passion to live, the hunger to survive, ran strong. The thought of death was bitter; yet the surrender of power was more bitter still.

I looked at the tall figure standing there in the slanting rain, as though I had seen it for the first time. It took on a pathos that made me forget even its sullenness, its malignity, its envenomed and useless spirit. For some power within me, some rudimentary force not altogether myself, told me it was too late to draw back.

"*You're going to shoot!*" gasped the man on the coping-stones, as he peered out from under his sodden and dripping hat-brim and read some new determination on my face.

We looked at each other in silence. The drifting rain fell between us, pattering on the tin of the roof. It made a mournful sound as it fell. We seemed alone on the forlornest ridge of the world.

The man moved his lips, as though about to speak. Then he stopped. Something on his face made me wheel about sharply. I knew it was not a trick; for it was more than simulation I saw in his terrified eyes.

Then, as I looked, I saw an arm protrude from behind a smoke-stained chimney, between the two roofs on my left. Then appeared a head, a hatless head, with a white and angular face, swollen on one side. I did not notice the blue-barrelled revolver in his hand until he took aim. Then I turned again quickly, for he was aiming directly at Miron, the man on the coping-stone. And the face behind the steadying revolver barrel was the face that had been bruised and stunned by the huge fist of Miron himself, in the shadow of the bank-pillars on the street below.

I saw that same huge fist clutch at the air, even before the malicious crack of the cartridge smote on my ear; I saw him waver on the wet ledge for one brief second, and then topple over and outward into space. And with him, as he fell, fell the black valise.

In that brief heart-beat or two all my past life seemed to flash before my eyes. I seemed to see it all in one comprehensive vista, with its corroding and wasted years, with its foolish and antlike efforts, its blind and useless evasions.

Then came the sudden rending of the universe. Some sentient spark of consciousness told me the detonation had come. But the spark went out, even as it spoke its message. It was engulfed by a vast sense of shock, by an ebbing and sinking down through gray mists, stippled with aureoles of scarlet light against a background of utter black. Then the scarlet lights faded away, point by point. Then the blackness itself was no longer blackness. There was nothing. Then even nothingness itself became annihilated.

VI

I opened my eyes languidly. Then I closed them again. I lay there, indifferent, motionless, for what seemed ages and ages. Then I heard sounds, thin and far-away sounds, that seemed to come closer and closer about me. So for the second time I opened my eyes to the ache of light that surrounded me.

I seemed to be in a world of whiteness, imprisoned and entombed in white. The walls were white. The figures drifting about me were white. The very bed on which I lay was all of white. And the fierce white of the window squares irritated me, angered me beyond endurance and reason.

Then, luckily, I must have fallen asleep again. For when I looked up once more I saw a woman bending over me. She, too, was in white. She wore a bibbed apron of white, and a ridiculous little white cap on her head, like a charlotte-russe turned upside down.

She dropped my wrist and looked down at me with what seemed a noiseless little laugh. Then she disappeared without a word. She came back again in time. I saw her write something on what seemed to be a chart. Then she came over to the bedside with a white bowl and a spoon.

It wasn't until she began to feed me, with the reassuring smile one might turn on a child, that I realised my head was swathed up like a Turk's, that my left arm was bandaged and held tight in splints, that something about my body was stiff and sore and numb.

I looked at the woman with the charlotte-russe cap. I wanted to tell her that the white bowl made my eyes ache. But it seemed too hard to explain. So I looked at her again instead of at the bowl.

"How long have I been here?" I asked after a struggle that must have taken up many minutes. I intended to speak clearly and confidently, for I felt it would be a surprise to her. But my voice, in some way, seemed nothing more than a thin and creaking skeleton of sound.

"How long have I been here?" I asked, making a second great effort that left me languid and indifferent as to what her answer might be.

"Longer than you'd imagine," she answered quietly.

"You mean *weeks*?" I next asked her.

She did not deny it. Instead she smoothed my pillows for me.

"You must not talk. You have to stay quiet, very quiet."

I had to stay quiet, I told myself. And I must have been asleep again before I knew it. For when I awakened two men were talking over my bed.

"This is the Bromig case," said the more guttural voice—"the most confoundedly pertinacious specimen since *I've* been here! A compound fracture of the humerus, a messed-up costal cartilage, three ribs out of business, head contusions, and more lacerations than you could shake a stick at! Then Bromig bumped into some old skull depression when he had him on the table!"

"You mean he trephined?" asked the higher-noted voice.

"Yes. You know how Bromig does love to houseclean when he gets a head like that!"

"So did the Peruvians in the valley of Yucay, when our forefathers were pounding each other with stone axes!"

"Oh, I know trepanning is prehistoric enough, but it's the psychology of the thing that bothers me! If we haven't got hold of as neat a case of disintegrated personality——"

I opened my eyes and looked up at the figure leaning over me, with a frown.

"*Hello*, Mister Man!" said the guttural-voiced stranger, a little startled. There was something about his overfriendly intimacy that I resented. It was about time, I felt, for me to assert my own individuality. I was sick of being looked over as if I were a specimen in a natural history museum.

"I don't know you!" I told the guttural-voiced stranger testily.

It angered me to feel that my voice was nothing more than a thin and quavering whine.

"But I know *you*!" retorted the stranger cheerily. "And, what's more, I like you. I can't help admiring you."

And he stood there wagging his head at me. He irritated me, so I closed my eyes.

Then I opened them again.

"Why do you admire me?" I peevishly and foolishly demanded.

"Because you're going to beat Flournoy and Weir Mitchell and the *Hanna* case and the whole shooting-match," the idiot openly exulted.

He made me tired, so I closed my eyes again. Then I suddenly remembered something, and opened them.

"Who's handling my division?" I asked in sudden terror.

The two men looked at each other. I could see them draw closer to the bed. The younger man started to speak, but the older man silenced him with a quick and peremptory move of the hand.

"What *is* your division?" he asked; and he seemed to be holding his breath as he waited for my answer. I had to think hard for a minute or two.

"The Middle Division."

"And what does that include?" he suggested.

"Everything between Hamilton and the Detroit River, with the Tunnel thrown in—everything going over that line from MacGuigan's special to the Komoka gravel empties!"

Again the two men looked at each other foolishly, and the shorter man began wagging his head once more. But all that loomed before me was the terrifying predicament that my whole Middle Division might have been left unguarded.

"Train-despatcher!" I heard one man whisper to the other. He said it as though there was something marvellous in such a discovery.

"Tell us what you remember about that division," he suggested, letting his fingers drop casually to my wrist, which they held for a minute or two.

"But is somebody on my key?" I insisted. I knew what it might mean—my being away.

"Everything's looked after," he assured me.

"Are you certain of that?"

He laughed a little as he held me down. "Keep still there," he commanded. "Of course I'm sure of it."

"Tell us how this key trouble began," broke in the other man, a little impatiently.

I lay there thinking. It came back to me very slowly.

"Why, I switched from the Flint and Père Marquette and jumped over to the Grand Trunk. First I was at Strathroy, on the tunnel division, then they gave me a station at Chatham. Then they put me up at the Komoka Junction gravel-pits, to keep things straight when the double-tracking mess began. They knew I wanted to get on; they saw I was ready to *eat* hard work!"

"Yes—go on!"

"They found out that I could do good, clean operating. So they boosted me up to night-despatcher at London 'The Little.' "

"And——?" prompted my questioner.

I had to stop and think hard.

"Oh, yes!—The same night the boys wired that promotion down to my little wooden side-station by the gravel-pit, a hobo who'd dropped off a C. & G.T. beef car raided my ticket-office till."

"You mean this man broke in and robbed you?"

"Yes, he must have broken in to rob me. But I caught him—yes—I caught him at it and we had it hot and heavy—the tramp and me—all over the plantation!"

I could see one man catch at the other's sleeve as he emitted a whispered and anxious "Go on!"

"We fought like wildcats. He pounded me on the head with a coupling-pin. But I stuck to him, and a track walker came in and helped me tie him down. . . . The division superintendent read the story somewhere. He told the boys I was the right stuff and that he was going to push me. Seven weeks after he'd given me the night-despatching at London he made me chief day-despatcher for the whole Middle Division. They were still balled up with their double-tracking. And the new night-operator couldn't keep up the pace. So I jumped in an hour or two earlier to help him out, and got away an hour or two later. My head began bothering me a little, where that yeggman had hit me. Then I got so I couldn't sleep. Then I remember pounding the brass like mad one night, and it struck me as funny, and I began to laugh!"

That was as far as I could go. I stopped to rest; but the two men still waited without moving. The nurse with the charlotte-russe cap came to the bedside, but the older man waved her away with an angry sweep of the hand.

"And when you began to laugh?" he prompted me, as he might have prompted a three-year-old child.

"Then the man on the wire beside me looked up and listened to my 'send.' Then he made one leap, and screamed for help. I can remember that plainly. 'The wire—the wire!' he hollered. 'Get him off the wire! He's gone crazy—he's throwing number Twelve head-on into Twenty-One!'"

One of the men stirred uneasily. Then he turned and motioned for a passing nurse.

"For the love of Heaven, get Bromig here!" said the other man, looking about. Then he turned back and again motioned for me to go on.

"I can remember they got me away and quieted down, and then cut in on every wire they could get hold of, trying to save those two trains. I remember Miller, the new night-man. He sat down and bawled like a baby when they wired in it was all right, and number Twelve with her five sleepers was side-tracked at Glencoe."

"And what came after that?" asked one of the men.

I lay there thinking. There was nothing after that. And I was tired.

"What then?" demanded the guttural voice again.

"Then I woke up here," I told him, peevishly. The man was rubbing his hips with the palms of his hands, joyously.

"Won't Bromig wallow in this?" he murmured mysteriously. "Seven whole years—seven years of being *somebody else*—seven years of crawling around with a broken soul that was never properly set, and then to have the thing *broken and reset as straight as a die*!"

I was too tired to listen to his maunderings. I wanted to sleep.

"But which *one* of him is going to live?" asked the thin-noted voice, in what seemed an awed whisper.

"The right one!" exulted the other man. Something in his voice made me open my eyes again. He had stepped back, and was motioning toward a girl in furs, who stood at the door with an armful of roses, just behind the nurse with the charlotte-russe cap. I could see that she was a young woman, and that she had a great deal of dark brown hair.

I closed my eyes and opened them again, for the girl was leaning over the bed, looking down at me. She seemed to know me. She seemed nearer to me, in some way, than the others in that place of aching whiteness.

I looked up at her for a long, long time. But, try as I might, I could not remember. I shut my eyes tight, and once more tried to think.

"Don't you know me? Don't you remember?" asked the girl, bending lower over the bed. She seemed hurt. Her voice quavered a little.

"Can't you even remember that day you helped——"

She broke off and drew back, wounded in spirit, I felt.

"Try your name!" suggested the doctor beside her, in a whisper.

"I'm Margaret Shaler—Can't you even remember *that*?" she asked, a little forlornly.

"No," I told her.

"Give him time—give him time!" warned the guttural-voiced man.

"*But you don't remember?*" half-whispered the white-faced girl above me. Her mournful eyes looked down at me like stars out of an evening sky. They brought a sense of quiet and contentment to my troubled mind.

"Give him time!" explained the guttural voice, more gently than before.

Then I wondered why my hand that lay outside the coverlet was wet. I looked at it. They were tears. The girl leaning over the bed was crying, for some reason, against her will. I could feel her hand creep into mine.

Our two hands lay together, the one clutching and holding the other. I scarcely knew why, but it made me feel very happy. It made me hope for life again. It seemed to send a current of something warm and mysterious through all my body as I fell asleep. But I felt sorry I could not remember.